mug. He headed for the table . . . Pike looked up. His eyes narrowed.

Longarm never did know how he gave himself away, but Pike caught on that he was a target before Longarm had taken three steps. Pike grabbed the underside of the flimsy card table and heaved. Cards and drinks flew. Pike ducked behind the overturned table, dropping out of Longarm's sight. When he popped back into view, he had a revolver in his hand.

The bastard wasted no time with warnings. He triggered a shot across the room, and immediately ducked out of sight again. Someone behind Longarm screamed. Men scattered and glassware flew.

Longarm held his fire. He had no target.

A gun hand appeared over the top rim of the table and triggered another wild, unaimed shot in Longarm's general direction. Pike fired again, the slug striking somewhere behind the bar. Glassware shattered—bottles, glasses, the mirror . . .

Longarm didn't want any more bystanders hit . . . and that tabletop damn sure was not thick enough to stop a .44 caliber slug. He judged where Sidney Pike's chest would likely be, aimed, and fired . . .

TABOR EVANS

LONGARM

AND THE MISSING BRIDE

J

JOVE BOOKS, NEW YORK

THE BERKLEY PUBLISHING GROUP
Published by the Penguin Group
Penguin Group (USA) Inc.
375 Hudson Street, New York, New York 10014, USA
Penguin Group (Canada), 90 Eglinton Avenue East, Suite 700, Toronto, Ontario M4P 2Y3, Canada
(a division of Pearson Penguin Canada Inc.)
Penguin Books Ltd., 80 Strand, London WC2R 0RL, England
Penguin Group Ireland, 25 St. Stephen's Green, Dublin 2, Ireland (a division of Penguin Books Ltd.)
Penguin Group (Australia), 250 Camberwell Road, Camberwell, Victoria 3124, Australia
(a division of Pearson Australia Group Pty. Ltd.)
Penguin Books India Pvt. Ltd., 11 Community Centre, Panchsheel Park, New Delhi—110 017, India
Penguin Group (NZ), 67 Apollo Drive, Rosedale, North Shore 0632, New Zealand
(a division of Pearson New Zealand Ltd.)
Penguin Books (South Africa) (Pty.) Ltd., 24 Sturdee Avenue, Rosebank, Johannesburg 2196,
South Africa

Penguin Books Ltd., Registered Offices: 80 Strand, London WC2R 0RL, England

This is a work of fiction. Names, characters, places, and incidents either are the product of the author's
imagination or are used fictitiously, and any resemblance to actual persons, living or dead, business
establishments, events, or locales is entirely coincidental.

LONGARM AND THE MISSING BRIDE

A Jove Book / published by arrangement with the author

PRINTING HISTORY
Jove edition / March 2009

Copyright © 2009 by Penguin Group (USA) Inc.
Cover illustration by Miro Sinovcic.

ISBN: 978-0-515-14595-3

JOVE®
Jove Books are published by The Berkley Publishing Group,
a division of Penguin Group (USA) Inc.,
375 Hudson Street, New York, New York 10014.
JOVE® is a registered trademark of Penguin Group (USA) Inc.
The "J" design is a trademark of Penguin Group (USA) Inc.

PRINTED IN THE UNITED STATES OF AMERICA

10 9 8 7 6 5 4 3 2 1

Chapter 1

Custis Long stopped in the middle of a tree-shaded block south of Denver's Colfax Avenue. He took his time about lighting a cheroot, making no attempt to hide the fact that he was eyeing a pair of women who were window-shopping outside a ladies' ready-to-wear. A mother and daughter most likely, both very pretty. Both reasonably fashionable. Both with full but nicely shaped figures. He decided he would not mind having either of them. Or both. At the same time.

That thought brought a wicked grin to his face as he visualized these two very proper ladies naked and twined together like a nest of snakes.

The older woman saw his expression. She clouded up and looked like she intended to rain all over him. She set her mouth in a pout and approached him.

"You're staring at us why are you peering at us that way are you a masher young man mind your manners or I shall call a policeman."

"I'm impressed," he drawled.

That took her somewhat aback. "What?"

He took the cheroot from his lips and touched the brim

1

of his snuff brown Stetson hat. "I said that I'm impressed, ma'am. You got that out without hardly stopping to breathe." His grin returned.

"I meant what I said. I could call a policeman."

"Easily done, ma'am. I *am* a policeman. Well, sort of. I'm a deputy United States marshal." He removed the Stetson and made a bow toward her. "Deputy Custis Long at your service, ma'am."

"Oh." She blushed. "I suppose I was a little . . . abrupt . . . just now, I mean."

"No need t' apologize, ma'am. D'you still need my services? How can I help you?"

"I just thought you were looking at us, you see, and . . ." The lady's voice trailed away. She obviously did not know where that thought was taking her.

"Why, ma'am," Longarm said, "indeed I was lookin' at you. How could I not? Beautiful morning. Beautiful ladies, both o' you. I apologize if I distressed you, but I couldn't help but to admire you an' your friend. Or sister, is it, the two of you havin' the same hair color an' set of features?"

"She is my daughter, but I thank you for that compliment. You say you are a deputy?"

"Yes, ma'am, an' if you ever need anybody arrested, you jus' come see me about it." He laughed.

"I think . . . I think we should go now."

"As you wish, ma'am, but I must say you've brightened my morning an' got this week off to a fine start."

The lady blushed—and what could *she* have been thinking to prompt such a display—and scurried back to her daughter, grabbing the younger woman by the elbow and dragging her into the shop.

Longarm smiled, then carefully adjusted the set of his

2

Stetson and headed on toward Colfax Avenue and the Federal Building.

Custis Long never quite understood the snake charmer's effect he often had on women. He certainly did not consider himself to be all that handsome. Interesting perhaps. But not handsome.

He was tall, several inches over six feet, and lean, with broad shoulders and narrow hips. He had brown hair and a huge sweep of dark brown handlebar mustache. His face was tanned from long exposure to the elements.

The man known as Longarm wore a brown tweed coat over a calfskin vest with a gold watch chain hanging across his flat belly, a string tie, striped trousers, and calf-high black cavalry boots.

He carried a double-action Colt .44 in a black leather cross-draw rig. And at one end of the watch chain was a .44-caliber derringer.

At the moment, he was on his way to the office of U.S. Marshal William Vail. He had just come from a pleasant breakfast with an old friend. Longarm and Jack Boggs cowboyed together in the days before Longarm took an oath to serve as a deputy to Billy Vail. Now Longarm's belly was full, those ladies were lovely, and he was ready for . . . well, for damn near anything.

He reached Colfax, turned toward the newly risen sun, and quickly strode the three blocks to the tall, gray granite mausoleum that passed for Denver's federal office building.

Despite the early hour, Billy Vail's clerk, Henry, already had the office open and was busy behind his desk.

"Mornin', Henry. Is the boss in?"

"Not yet. Good morning, Custis. No, don't bother taking your hat off. You won't be here that long."

"Got something for me already?"

"Something easy this time," the mild-looking bespectacled clerk said.

"Funny thing. I've heard that before," Longarm told him.

"Yes, but this time it's true. I have a bunch of subpoenas for you to service. Judge Herndon's clerk brought them over."

"Interesting cases?"

"Not especially." Henry riffled through some of the papers on his desk, obviously the Notices to Appear that Longarm would have to deliver. "Penny-ante cases actually. Gambling on an Indian reservation. Attempt to defraud by mail. Illegal manufacture of whiskey." He shook his head. "Like I said, nothing really interesting. But it all has to be done, and you are just the boy who can do it. I have faith in you, Custis. Billy has faith in you. We know you won't let us down." Henry grinned and picked up the stack of forms, each already signed with all proper stamps and seals affixed. "Here y'go, Longarm. Have fun with them."

Longarm sighed. Not all law enforcement work was exciting. He had certainly learned that over the years. He turned toward the door.

"Wait a minute," Henry said. "Let me give you some vouchers for travel and meals."

Longarm lifted an eyebrow in inquiry.

"These are mostly down around Colorado City and up into the Bayou Salade. It will probably be best to take the train down to Colorado Springs and hire a horse there."

"Good, because the last horse the damned army loaned me had a mouth made of cast iron and the disposition of a rattlesnake. How much time do I have?"

"The court dates aren't until next month or after."

Longarm grinned but said nothing. He collected the

4

paperwork, bade Henry a cheerful good-bye, and headed toward his boardinghouse where he kept a bag always packed with the essentials . . . like cheroots, rye whiskey, and .44 cartridges.

Chapter 2

The train arrived in Colorado Springs promptly at 12:35 P.M. Longarm stepped down to the platform, pausing to offer a helping hand to a girl in her teens with pimples. She had been surreptitiously observing him ever since they left Monument. And blushing every time she lowered those big, blue eyes. He would have liked to know just what the girl was imagining when she did that. Hell, it might have made *him* blush.

He bowed and touched the brim of his Stetson, then ambled off down the platform to collect his carpetbag and saddle from the luggage car. By the time he had his things together and another cheroot fired up, most of the crowd had cleared away.

Longarm looked over the three hansom cabs that remained nearby. He chose the second in line, the one with the best cared for horse. The animal was not large but it was clean, the hoofs were polished, and the mane and tail nicely trimmed. It would do. He tossed his gear into the coach and nodded to the driver, an aging man who could have used some of the grooming that his horse received.

"Where to, neighbor?"

"Colorado City, if you please."

"And if I don't?"

Longarm shrugged. "I can take another cab." The town, older than Colorado Springs, was four miles west. He reached inside for his saddle and bag.

"Hey, I was just jawing. I'll take you wherever you want."

"Then make it Colorado City. The Washburn House."

The driver raised an eyebrow. "Are you sure Miz Washburn will take you? She's choicy about the guests she'll accept."

"She'll accept me." Longarm grinned. "Trust me."

"If you say so. But if you don't mind, I'll wait outside for a bit till I see do you need a second ride someplace."

"That's fine by me. How much for the first ride?"

"Fifty cents."

"And if I was some poor cowhand, what would it be?"

The driver chuckled. "Fifty cents. But I might be talked into taking more if more was offered."

"Not much chance of that, I think." Longarm returned his things inside the cab and climbed in behind them. He barely had time to get settled on the seat before he heard the driver's whip snap and the outfit lurched forward. Half an hour later, he was tugging the bellpull at Mae Washburn's front door.

A thirteen-year-old girl in freckles and pigtails answered his ring. Her face split in a wide smile when she saw him. "Uncle Custis! What are you doing here?"

"I'm a weary traveler lookin' for a place t' lay his head," Longarm said.

"You found it," Tina Washburn yelped, pushing the door open to admit him. Once the door was closed and they were out of sight of the neighbors, she squealed again and threw her arms around him. "Are you going to marry me this trip, Uncle Custis?"

"Can't," he said, his hug lifting her completely off the floor. "I'm on duty."

"Next time then," Tina said, laughing.

"Do you have room for me?"

"If we didn't, Mama would throw somebody out in the street to make room for you. You know that."

"Where is your mom anyway?"

"She's at the greengrocer's getting stuff for dinner tonight. She'll be back soon. We can sit in the parlor and spoon while we wait for her."

"Don't tempt me. Why, you're becoming positively beautiful, do you know that?"

"I know that I'm knobby-kneed and homely, but Mama says I'll be a real head-turner one of these days."

"I say it, too."

"And we'll get married then."

"Absolutely," Longarm told her.

The girl hugged him again, then jumped back. "Oh! I forgot. I have biscuits in the oven." She turned and started loping toward the kitchen. "Take your regular room. You know where."

Longarm was smiling when he mounted the staircase to the second floor. It was nice to be back to a place where he was welcome.

Chapter 3

"I'm done," Longarm said, "cash me out, please." He pushed his meager pile of chips toward the dealer, a woman with brassy blond hair and tits that threatened to pop out of her blouse. Not that anyone would have minded if they did.

The woman exchanged the chips for coins and in a bored tone said, "Move along, cowboy. Let someone else have the chair."

Longarm grunted and pocketed the coins without counting them. He knew close enough what would be there. The dealer had clipped him for a quarter. He saw her do it. Fine, he figured. He had intended to tip her a half buck. Now she could settle for the quarter she swiped. He got up and left the table, paused for one more rye at the bar, then walked the two blocks back to Mae's house.

There was no sign of the other three boarders when he got there. Apparently, they had gone off to bed. Tina was in the parlor studying, and the house girl had been sent home for the night. Mae was alone in the kitchen. Longarm crept up behind her and wrapped his arms around her. He bent down and nibbled her earlobe.

"Damn you, Custis. You think you can come in here like

this. Not a word from you in I don't know how long. Now you think you can just . . . God, you know how horny that makes me. Now stop!"

"D'you really want me to?"

"No, damn you." Mae turned around in his embrace and put her arms around him. "You know that you can get away with anything, you bastard."

"Hush, you don't want Tina hearing you use language like that."

"I don't want her to walk in here and catch us together either."

He released Mae and stepped back half a pace, his eyes ranging over her. He liked what he saw.

Mae Washburn was almost as tall as Longarm. She was a full-figured filly with coppery red hair and more freckles than her daughter had. She had huge gray-green eyes with deep laugh lines at the corners. Longarm had known the two of them since Tina was a pup.

"Tina already put a pitcher of water in your room and a pail of hot water, too, in case you want to wash off. Go on upstairs. I'll be along as soon as Tina goes to bed. Leave your door unlocked."

Longarm nodded, glanced over his shoulder to make sure Tina was not watching, then gave Mae a soft, lingering kiss: "Later," he said.

He lay on top of the covers, naked, his dick standing tall. His eyes were tightly closed and he feigned sleep.

He heard the faint click of the doorknob being turned and the latch opening, then felt the soft flow of cool air as the door silently swung open.

Floorboards creaked and the bedsprings groaned as another person joined him on the bed. Longarm could not resist a hint of a smile as he felt first the cool brush of a woman's hair tickling his thighs, and then the warm touch of a tongue on his balls.

A hand slipped between his legs and gently prodded them to part. Longarm complied, spreading wide so the mobile tongue could reach his asshole and rim him, then glide back up onto his balls. Mae sucked his balls into her mouth, first one and then the other. Longarm reached down and stroked the back of her head.

He guided her mouth up onto his cock, where she sucked and licked, noisily slurping.

She peeled back his foreskin and ran the tip of her tongue around and around the head of his cock, then took it deep into her mouth and sucked all the harder.

"If you don't stop that damn soon," he whispered, "you're gonna get a mouthful."

"I already have a mouthful," she mumbled.

"You know what I mean. I'll squirt down your throat."

Mae's response was to suck even harder.

Longarm had not been lying. Within seconds, he stiffened and tried to stifle an impulse to cry out as the sweet flow of juice shot out of his cock.

Mae clamped her lips tight around him and struggled to swallow all of the flow. She gagged twice as the volume of his juice threatened to overwhelm her, but she stayed with him and continued to suck—and to swallow—until he was done.

Then she sat up, grinning, and wiped her chin and mouth with the back of her hand.

Longarm chuckled. "Have I ever mentioned t' you, ma'am, that you are one helluva fine landlady?"

Mae laughed. "Welcome home, cowboy. What else can I do for you?"

"For openers, you can set there an' let me look at you for a few minutes. There's not many women get better looking the less they have on. You're prettiest when you're naked."

"And after that?"

"After that, you'd best lay down here beside me 'cause tonight I figure t' become a farmer."

Mae raised an eyebrow. "Whatever do you mean by that?"

"I mean, ma'am, I intend t' plow your patch this whole night long. Now come here, please. I'm wantin' to kiss you."

He did not have to ask twice.

Chapter 4

Longarm felt good in the morning. Tired, but good. He washed again—he felt sticky and needed it—then dressed and went down to breakfast.

He had gotten damned little sleep the night before. Mae must have gotten none at all because when he got to the kitchen, she already had a pan of biscuits and two fresh pies out of the oven.

He wanted to grab her and shove his tongue down her throat—it had been there already, of course, and certain other highly interesting places as well—but the boarders were in the dining room and Tina was fluttering in and out of the kitchen. He did give Tina a kiss and a hug, a much more sedate and fatherly gesture than he would have liked to give her mother.

"Mornin', Miz Washburn. Mornin', Tina."

"Good morning, Uncle Custis. Go ahead and sit down. I'll bring your coffee."

Longarm took his time with breakfast. There would have been no point to walking into town before the shopkeepers opened their doors. About eight o'clock he polished off a final cup of coffee, lit a cheroot, and strolled down to Colorado City's main street.

He crossed over the trolley tracks, stepped around two piles of horse apples, and found Fulbright's Mercantile, Mining Supplies Our Specialty. A tiny bell mounted over the door tinkled when he went inside. A moment later, a middle-aged man in sleeve garters emerged from a back room.

"Help you, sir?"

Longarm glanced down at the subpoena Henry had given him, then said, "I'm looking for a gentleman named Ford Leopold Fargo."

"I'm Leo Fargo. What can I do for you?"

"You're being served notice to show up as a material witness in a case against a fellow named, uh, Bertil Doupis." He scowled. "Is that right?"

Fargo laughed. "Yeah, that's right. Bert sold me some stuff. Some other fella claimed he stole it. I don't know anything about that, though."

"All they want is for you to show up and answer some questions. Your travel and meals will be provided. The particulars are on here." Longarm handed him the subpoena. "Exactly where and when . . . it's all there."

Fargo shrugged. "I got no problem with that. Now I have a question for you. Is your name Long?"

"Yeah, but how would you know that?"

"Because I have a message for you. A kid from Western Union came in just as I was closing up yesterday afternoon. He left an envelope for you." Fargo bent down and rummaged under his counter for a moment, then stood up with a bright yellow envelope in hand. "Here 'tis."

"Thanks."

Longarm carried the message outside before he opened

it. Whatever it was, he was sure it would not be good news. And it pretty much had to come from the office since Billy Vail and Henry were the only ones who would know where to find him.

He read the wire quickly, then spat, "Shit!" loudly enough to draw a scowl of censure from a woman walking on the other side of the street.

"Shit," he grumbled again. But not quite so loudly this time.

Chapter 5

"I have t' go over to the Springs," Longarm complained to Mae.

"What's wrong with that? It's a nice town." She smiled. "And they have some wonderful places there to have lunch. Would you like for me to ride along with you? You could pay for the pleasure of my company by buying me lunch."

"Me, too?" Tina put in.

"Both o' you calm down. Much as I'd enjoy spending the day with you two, this is serious business."

"What is?"

"This . . . dammit, I don't know yet. That's the whole point. I'm s'posed to go over there an' get filled in on the assignment by Acting Sheriff E. David Agnew."

"And what is wrong with that, pray tell?"

"E. David is an assho—" He blinked and looked over at Tina, then modified his choice of intended words. "The man is a horse's patoot, that's what's wrong with it. He's a politician, not a lawman, an' my experience with politicians don't show them t' be worth a da . . . darn. Whatever the man wants, he'll figure some way for it to feather his own nest. It won't have nothing t' do with enforcing the laws."

19

"But your boss says you have to go?"

Longarm nodded. "He does."

"Then what will you do?"

"I'll go, of course. But that don't mean I have t' like it."

Longarm went upstairs, got his gear, and came back down to the foyer where both Mae and Tina were waiting for him. "Do you have to stay, Uncle Custis?" Tina asked, eyeing his saddle and bag.

"I don't know. Tell you what. If I can, I'll come back here."

"You could leave your things here. That way you'd have to come back."

Longarm smiled down at the kid. "If I can I will. But I have t' be prepared for whatever comes."

"Promise?"

"Promise," he assured her.

Longarm stood for a moment looking at Mae until Tina said, "Oh, go ahead and kiss her. I know you want to. And she wants you to. I'll leave the room if it makes you feel any better."

Tina gave Longarm a hug and got a kiss on the forehead, then scampered off toward the kitchen. As soon as she was out of sight, Longarm did his best to lick Mae's tonsils.

"Now that," he said when they broke the clinch, "is sure t' bring me back soon as I can."

"Any time. You know that."

He kissed her again, then took his things and set off in search of a hansom to carry him the few miles to the county courthouse in Colorado Springs.

Chapter 6

Construction was not yet completed on the courthouse, so Longarm had to track down the temporary offices of the acting sheriff. He found the building he wanted, located Agnew's office, and presented himself. Reluctantly.

The sheriff's greeting was curt. "Why did they send you?"

Longarm looked down at the thin, dapper, overdressed son of a bitch who sat behind the big desk. "You want somebody else, I can go back t' what I was doing," he snapped.

"Vail sent you?"

"I damn sure wouldn't be here for any other reason."

"Very well then. Beggars can't be choosers."

"Thanks for that vote of confidence," Longarm said.

"The problem is this," Agnew told him. "We received a tip that Horace Brightley may be kidnapped tomorrow. Do you know Brightley?"

"Never heard o' the man."

"Horace Brightley owns two gold mines in the Fairplay district. I understand he may be negotiating to buy a third. Tomorrow he will take a coach through Ute Pass to South Park and on to Fairplay. My tip suggests the coach may be waylaid and Mr. Brightley robbed of the considerable sum of cash he will be carrying as a down payment on that purchase. He may also be kidnapped and held for further ransom. Or not. My information is unclear about that."

"None o' that would violate federal law," Longarm reminded him. "Robbery an' kidnapping ain't against the U.S. statutes."

"I was just getting to the question of jurisdiction, damn it. Be quiet and let me finish."

Longarm scowled. And shut his mouth. In addition to a wonderfully arrogant disposition, E. David Agnew had asshole buddies in both Denver and Washington. Crossing the man would be pleasant . . . but not sensible.

"Any competent local authority may request assistance from federal officers. It says that quite clearly in the statutes. Besides which, the Fullbright and Greenleaf Express Company has a contract to carry the United States mail. That means any robbery of their coaches could be considered a mail robbery whether or not a mail pouch is actually taken. Under either of those terms, I placed my request for assistance before Marshal William Vail. He sent"—Agnew frowned—"you.

"I have written down the pertinent information for you. You, um, are able to read at a fourth-grade level or better, aren't you?"

Longarm declined to answer. He did, however, accept the carefully lettered sheet that the acting sheriff handed him. Damn, he hoped Agnew did not get the permanent appointment for which he was lobbying the governor's office.

"Tomorrow, you said."

"It is all written down there."

"Right. Thanks."

Longarm got the hell out of there. He retrieved his gear

22

from the outer office and headed for the Fullbright and Greenleaf Express Company depot just west of the railroad station.

He checked the F & G schedule, then grabbed a hansom and headed back to Mae's house. The stagecoach with Brightley aboard would not be leaving until tomorrow morning. That gave Longarm one more night with his two favorite females in this county.

While he rode, he pondered. It was unlike E. David Agnew to give up any chance for glory, especially something that would both earn him a rich and powerful new friend in Horace Brightley and make him look good for the governor.

As they were pulling to a halt in front of the Washburn House, the reason struck him and he had to shake his head in sheer admiration.

If Longarm fucked up, Agnew could blame him. And the United States marshal's office.

If Longarm saved Brightley's bacon, Agnew could crow about it as resulting from his information and his close cooperation with those wonderful U.S. deputies.

Asshole!

Longarm crawled out of the cab, paid the driver, and retrieved his things. He was smiling when he mounted the steps to the front porch. He had another evening playing Parcheesi with Tina to look forward to. And another night with the child's mother.

Chapter 7

Longarm saw Tina off to school the next morning, then stepped back inside the vestibule where the neighbors could not see and gave Mae a long, lingering kiss. "Thanks for letting me leave my stuff here." He did not want to be encumbered with luggage on this trip.

"I'm happy to do it," Mae told him. "It guarantees you will come back to see me."

Longarm smiled. "I'd do that anyway an' you know it. One more kiss now an' I gotta go."

"I will pray for your safety."

He did not know quite how to respond to that, so he gave her another brief kiss and left.

On his way to the Fullbright and Greenleaf Express depot, he stopped first at the town marshal's office.

"H'lo, Tom. Can I ask a favor of you?"

"You can ask, Longarm. Hell, I might even say yes. If you buy me a beer," the Colorado City lawdog told him.

"I'll have to owe you the beer. Right now, I got t' catch a stage up the pass."

Tom Eason glanced at the big Regulator clock on the wall and said, "You have time if the favor doesn't take too long. The coach should be pulling in from the Springs in fifteen minutes or so. That's a short leg, so they're generally spot on time."

"What I need from you, Tom, is the loan of one of your scatterguns. You got something short an' nasty?"

"Of course I do. How about a double gun with ten-inch barrels and a cut-down stock? I like to carry it slung on a thong over my shoulder. If you wear a duster, you can carry it and nobody will see a thing until you want them to."

"Great," Longarm said. "But that brings up a second favor. You got a duster I can wear today?"

Eason nodded. "Hell, I'll even throw in a pocket full of single-aught shells. I favor the single over double-aught. Doesn't carry quite as far, but there's more lead balls in the load, and a sawed-off shotgun is for close work anyhow."

"Single will be fine," Longarm said.

"Come along then. Let's get you outfitted. Do you, uh, want any help with whatever you're doing?"

Longarm shook his head. "It would take you way the hell out o' your jurisdiction. Besides, a show of force might just scare away the robbers until another time. I'd rather nail them while I have the chance. Thanks for the offer, though, Tom. I truly appreciate it."

"You've done more than enough to help me in the past," Eason said over his shoulder as he unlocked his gun cabinet.

"One fare to Fairplay," Longarm told the F & G ticket clerk. He had the right to free passage simply by displaying his badge, but a hunch told him it might be sensible to board the coach as just another traveler.

"Twelve dollars, please."

Longarm paid and went outside to wait. He did not have

long to stand under the overhang where the coach would stop. It arrived on time, a light rig pulled by four high-stepping horses rather than one of the heavy Concord-style stagecoaches. Those would simply be too much weight to drag up and down the mountain, and would require a six-horse hitch at the very least, maybe more on some of the uphill pulls.

There were four passengers already in the coach, plus the jehu on the box. Longarm had no trouble at all deciding which of his traveling companions would be Horace Brightley.

Brightley had steel gray hair and a carefully groomed mustache. His suit probably cost more than Longarm earned in a year's time. He was traveling with two items that he seemed to value highly: one a shiny valise big enough to hold a small fortune in bank notes, the other an equally shiny red-haired young woman who appeared to be permanently attached to the man's arm.

The redhead was wearing makeup, but so skillfully applied that Longarm had difficulty deciding for sure whether she wore it. Not that he minded taking time to work that question out. The girl was first class. And no doxy. This one was a gem.

Another gentleman—Longarm pegged him as a bodyguard—wore a cheap suit and a scowl. He kept giving Longarm suspicious glares, and early on managed to jostle Longarm's side. Checking for weapons most likely. Longarm thought, but was not entirely sure, that the bodyguard was not aware of the scattergun carried under his left arm.

The last passenger was a seedy, raggedly dressed fellow who looked like a miner coming off a drunk.

No introductions were offered and no one spoke other than the occasional " 'Scuse me" and "Sorry."

Horace Brightley and his party occupied the front-facing bench, which left the rearward-facing seat for Longarm and the miner.

Longarm handed the driver his ticket and the jehu climbed back onto the box. Seconds later, the driver's whip cracked and the coach lurched forward, the iron tires grinding loudly on the cinders and gravel of the city's streets.

Longarm slumped in his corner and half closed his eyes. If someone wanted to assume he was asleep, that would be just fine.

Chapter 8

Longarm half expected the holdup to occur when the coach made the first rest stop where the team would be exchanged. He was primed and ready when the jehu called down, "Ten minutes, folks. Time enough to grab a sandwich if you want one."

Brightley's party climbed down to the ground, the bodyguard first, then the redhead, and finally the great man himself. The ragged miner stayed put. Longarm got out.

The stop was made at a community—it was far from being large enough or settled enough to be a town—called Florissant. It consisted of a store with a sagging roof, the stagecoach relay barn, and two houses. A few more scattered houses could be seen in the distance.

"There's food and drink in the store there for them as wants, but don't be late. When this coach is ready, we pull out," the driver announced, "with you or without you."

The F & G hostler and a boy of ten or eleven brought the fresh team out already wearing harness. They and the driver pitched in to remove the tired horses that had made the slow, difficult climb up Ute Pass and to hitch the fresh animals.

Longarm stood leaning against a fence rail as if stretching his legs. He kept watching for trouble but none came. It could well be, he thought, that E. David Agnew's tip was baseless. That would leave Billy Vail and his deputy with egg on their faces, but E. David untouched. For a snake, the man was a clever son of a bitch, Longarm conceded. Shit, he almost hoped there would be a robbery attempt so he could foil it and Billy Vail could get credit for the success.

Once the new team was in place—more like twenty minutes than ten, not that it mattered—the jehu called a warning to his passengers, then held the door while everyone boarded.

"Go ahead," the burly bodyguard said when Longarm tried to hold back and be the last one in. The bodyguard was not being polite; the man simply did not want to turn his back on someone he did not know.

Longarm climbed in ahead of him and resumed his seat beside the miner, who had begun to snore.

The coach rocked on its leather suspension and began to roll forward again.

"Why are we stopping?" the bodyguard asked an hour later when they pulled off the road.

"I take it you have not traveled this route before," Brightley told him. "There is a steep downgrade ahead. The driver will chain a log drag behind the coach to keep it from riding up on the horses' hocks. They do it every trip. The express company keeps a supply of drags piled here for them to use."

Brightley turned his attention to his red-haired companion and in a much warmer voice said, "There is a wonderful view from this high point, Greta. You can stand here and see all of South Park spread out below you. The feeling is like being on top of the world. There should be enough daylight left for you to see it if you want to get out for a moment. I'm sure the driver will not mind."

"I'm comfortable where I am, Horace. Do I have to get out?"

"No, of course not. We'll stay right here then. This stop won't take long."

Longarm, like Brightley's bodyguard, kept looking out at both sides. Looking for trouble.

The sun was nearly down, dropping out of sight behind the next in the chain of north-south-running mountain ranges. It would be dark before they reached the rolling grassland that was the floor of South Park, Longarm figured. They were due in Fairplay around midnight.

The bodyguard grunted, and Longarm saw that the man's attention was focused on something off to his right, to Longarm's left. Longarm leaned forward and peered in that direction. A horse and rider came slowly out of the gathering dusk. No, two horses. One rider. Certainly it was no gang bent on thievery. In fact, the rider stopped his horses a good fifty yards distant and sat there. Looking out at the view of South Park? Perhaps.

Longarm heard a faint but unmistakably familiar click. A pistol hammer had been cocked.

The bodyguard heard it, too, and started to turn his head.

The man was too late.

A small-caliber pistol cracked and a lead pellet was driven into the bodyguard's head point-blank behind his ear.

The man's body jerked, already dead, and released a long, fluttering fart as taut muscles suddenly relaxed.

Longarm stared half in disbelief as the lovely redhead turned her little nickel-plated Sharps derringer toward Horace Brightley.

"Greta! I don't—I don't understan—"

"It's simple, sweetheart." She smiled. "This is my way of saying good-bye. Now hand me that bag, please, and I shall be on my way."

The rider had moved in close after Greta fired her pistol. Now he called, "Are you all right, doll?"

"I'm fine, honey. Everything is just fine."

"Okay, kill the old bastard and we'll be on our way."

"Turn around, Horace. I'll be careful. You won't feel a thing." Her voice was sweet as syrup.

"Greta, please, I—"

"Turn around, you old piece of shit, or I'll gut-shoot you and you'll take days to die. Now do it, damn you." She waved the little pistol at her lover. Former lover, Longarm supposed that would be now.

He could smell the sharp odor of spent gunpowder and the dank scent of the dead bodyguard's flatulence. And the stink of fear that suddenly was coming off Horace Brightley.

"The bag with the money in it," Greta snarled. "I want it. Right now."

Brightley looked like he was ready to cry. Not that the man could be blamed. Suddenly, he was losing the money, the girl, and even his life. Suddenly, he was losing everything.

"Greta. Please."

"Now. I won't tell you again."

"Hurry up, honey," the rider called from outside. "Shoot him and let's get out of here."

Longarm saw the girl change her grip on the Sharps so she could get her thumb over the hammer to cock it for another shot.

Outside the coach, her accomplice was preoccupied with the driver.

If Longarm intended to do anything about this, it was either now or never. And never mind the potential danger to Horace Brightley.

Chapter 9

There was no time to unbutton the linen duster. Longarm raised the twin muzzles of the sawed-off and tripped the front trigger.

Flame, smoke, and lead tore through the light cloth of the duster.

The plug of No. 0 buckshot, almost as compact as a single slug at this point-blank distance, struck the redhead at about throat level. At that range, the pellets hit with the impact of a tracklayer's single-jack. They tore her jaw completely off and ripped away most of her throat and neck.

For a few seconds there, the inside of the light coach was awash in smoke and splattering blood.

Bits of gristle and bone were blown onto the back of the coach seat, and a gaping hole was torn out of the back of the vehicle.

Greta simply ceased to exist. In that split second, she was no longer a person, much less a pretty young woman.

Horace Brightley caught a glimpse out of the corner of his eye and began throwing up.

In the meantime, Longarm heard the bark of two gunshots close beside him.

The accomplice!

He swiveled to face the rider, but too late.

The "drunken" miner had a short-barreled .45 in hand. It had appeared seemingly from nowhere. He was the one who had fired, and Greta's partner was already falling backward out of his saddle. The man hit the ground and did not even bounce, dead before he got there.

The miner swung around toward Longarm with the .45. "Who the hell are you?" he demanded.

"Me?" Longarm yelled back at him over the nearly deafening gunfire in closed quarters. "Who the fuck are *you*?"

"I'm the guy that's gonna shoot your hairy ass if you don't pretty quick explain," the miner said.

"Friend, that shooter o' yours ain't yet cocked. My L.C. Smith double-ten is. An' I ain't fired but one barrel so far. The other'n is aimed point-blank at your midsection and it'll give you one hell of a bellyache if anything happens t' make my trigger finger twitch. So let me ask this again. Who the hell are you?"

"All right. Wait a second. Just one second here."

Carefully, *very* carefully, the fellow transferred his revolver to his left hand, wrapping his fingers around the cylinder, not the grip. Then slowly, he reached inside his shirt.

Longarm tensed, still not sure if he would have to shoot the man. But he was serious about where the scattergun was pointing.

"Take a look here," the fellow said, pulling out a flat, brown leather wallet. He flipped it open to display a very small badge. "Pinkertons," he said.

"A Pink?"

The scruffy fellow nodded. "Aye, so I am. Now your turn, friend. Who would you be?"

"Deputy United States marshal," Longarm said.

"You got credentials?"

"I do."

"While you're getting them, you might pay some mind to your coat. It seems to be burning."

"Well, shit." Longarm half stood inside the confines of the coach. He ripped the front of the duster open, sending buttons flying. The Pink was right, though. The smoldering cloth had broken into active flame. Longarm took the duster off and threw it out of the coach window.

"Now about those credentials." the Pinkerton reminded him.

Longarm showed him. The fellow whistled when he read them. "Shit, you're Long?"

"That's right. Longarm to my friends."

"Well, I'm damned glad we're on the same side here. You're mighty quick with that scattergun."

"Which reminds me." Longarm carefully lowered the hammer over the unfired shell that remained in the gun.

The Pinkerton man grinned and returned his pistol beneath his coat. Then he stuck his hand forward to shake. "John Smith here. I know. It's my real name. And I'm pleased to make your acquaintance. Can I call you Longarm?"

"You damn sure can, John Smith, an' it's a pleasure for me t' know you, too. You did a nice job with that fella out there. But what about this man here?" Longarm asked, nodding toward the bodyguard Greta had murdered.

Brightley sat upright. He looked a little green. Except for all the bright red gore he wore where pieces of the late Greta had splattered.

Smith said, "He is . . . I mean to say he was . . . my partner. Albert Boatwright was his real name. Him and me was partners for the past three years or just shy of it. A good man, too. He didn't deserve what that greedy bitch gave him."

"I'm sorry, John. You were both Pinkertons then."

Smith nodded. "That's right. Mr. Brightley hired Pinkertons to guard him and all the cash he was carrying. Albert and me worked out between us that one should make himself known and the other stay in the shadows. So to speak. It's a trick we've pulled before. Albert always played it out front, him being so big and intimidating. I'd be a drunk or a prospector or sometimes a drifting cowboy. Whatever. This time . . . dammit, this time it didn't quite work out like it was supposed to."

"Are you all right, Mr. Brightley?" Longarm asked.

"I am . . . shocked. And I need a bath and a change of clothing, but I will be fine." He looked at what was left of the thing that had been his girlfriend and said, "Didn't she realize that I would have given her anything she asked for? I was in love with her. God help me, I was. Then she did . . . this." He gagged a little, the bile rising in his throat, but he swallowed it back and did not throw up any more.

"Is everyone all right in there?" the jehu called.

"Yeah, we are. How 'bout you?"

"That son of a bitch was going to shoot me," the driver said indignantly. "He said so. I believed him."

"Oh, I don't think he was lyin' to you." Longarm unlatched the coach door and climbed down to the ground. He turned back and said to Smith, "I'll trust you t' take Mr. Brightley the rest o' the way in to Fairplay."

"What about you?"

"I'm gonna catch up those loose horses and go back down the pass to Colorado City. I still got subpoenas t' serve." He reached into the coach and shook hands with Pinkerton Agent John Smith, touched the brim of his hat toward Horace Brightley, and turned to go look for the two straying horses before it became full dark.

Chapter 10

The night air at this elevation was cold and incredibly clear. Away from all the chimney smoke of the city, the air was as clear as springwater, and the stars presented a near solid blanket of tiny lights overhead.

There was more than enough light to travel by, but by the time Longarm reached the stagecoach relay station, he was shivering from the cold. He had not come prepared for this, and now even that half-burned duster he left behind back at the overlook would have been welcome.

Besides that, he was so tired he wanted to just lie down in the grass somewhere and snore. He had spent the previous night romping with Mae Washburn rather than wasting time sleeping. Now that indulgence was catching up with him.

When he reached the F & G barn, he unsaddled and turned the horses loose in the corral, threw a wad of hay in for them, and checked to make sure they had water. Once the animals were tended to, he walked over to the store and tried the door. It was not locked so he went inside.

The proprietor was tidying up. Longarm greeted him and asked, "Are you still open enough that I could get a bite to eat and somethin' to drink?"

"Oh, I suppose so. What would you like?"

"Almost anything that will fill my belly an' warm it."

"I got some pretty good whiskey that will sure warm your stomach and some leftover meat and biscuits that would fill it. They're cold, though, and I've already pulled the fire from the stove and cleaned out the ash. I wouldn't want to start a new one this late."

"That's fine. I don't need a hot meal, just a good one."

"Whiskey and supper, they'd be twenty-five cents each," the man said.

"That's fine." Longarm dug into his pocket and pulled out a silver cartwheel. "I'll take a dollar's worth if you please."

The storekeeper's interest perked up and he said, "For another fifty cents, I got a fat little Injun girl sleeping in the shed out back. Got a face that looks like she's been kicked by a mule . . . or maybe ought to be . . . but she bounces her ass pretty good."

"Thanks, but I'll make do with just the food an' the whiskey."

"Listen, if you have anything against fucking a Injun, mister, I got a daughter you could have for five dollars. White girl, mind you. A little soft in the head maybe, but you can't tell it so long as she keeps her mouth shut, and she isn't all that bad looking."

Longarm's face darkened with sudden fury. He grabbed the storekeeper by the front of his shirt and pulled the man close until they were nose to nose.

"You'd sell your own daughter, you piece o' shit?" he barked.

"M-m-mister, if a man sells any woman, he's selling somebody's daughter. There isn't all that much difference."

"I don't want the Indian. I don't want your daughter.

42

And I don't really much want the sight o' you. Now give me the food I already paid for and my whiskey."

Longarm was hoping the bastard would pour from a jug of homemade whiskey. Selling untaxed whiskey was a federal crime, and Longarm would damned sure arrest the man for it. The bottle he brought out had a label on it from a bonded distillery, though.

"Here, mister. Take this. Take the whole thing. And this pork. Biscuits. I got . . . there they are. Take them. No, take all of them. Please. Now just . . . go. Leave me be. I'm closed up for the night. This store is closed. You got to get out. Please."

Longarm took the chunk of greasy pork and handful of cold biscuits along with the bottle. He heard the bar being set in place over the door behind him.

With a sigh and a shiver, Longarm went back to the Fullbright and Greenleaf barn. He went inside to get a little shared warmth from the animals in the stalls there, and sat on an upended keg to eat his supper. When he was done with the food, he stepped outside to light a cheroot and work on the bottle of whiskey just a bit. He took the bottle with him when he crawled into the haystack, covering himself with the soft, aromatic loose hay in lieu of a blanket.

He had slept in worse beds.

Chapter 11

Longarm went straight to the Washburn House. He supposed he should turn these horses in to Sheriff E. David Agnew, but that could wait. He wanted a bath and a shave first, and a chance to change into some clean clothes.

He tied the animals—a surefooted brown and a handsome but stumble-footed black—to the fence in front of Mae's place and mounted the front porch. Before he had time to reach the door, it was flung open and a sobbing Mae rushed out and threw her arms around Longarm.

The woman was a mess. She was normally well groomed and tidy, but this afternoon her hair was in wild disarray. Her complexion was mottled in ugly shades of red. Tear tracks streaked her cheeks, and there were dark circles of sleeplessness under her haggard eyes.

"What the hell's wrong, Mae?"

"Custis, I'm so glad you're back. It's Tina, Custis."

"What . . . ?"

"She has been kidnapped. Custis, someone stole my baby. They took her, Custis."

"All right. Calm down an' get control o' yourself here." He took her by the shoulders, turned her around, and guided her indoors. He took her into the parlor and sat her down on a settee, then sat close beside her and put an arm around Mae's trembling shoulders. "Slowly now. Tell me."

"They took her."

"You said 'they.' As in more than one. D'you know who they are?"

"I . . . no. I don't know who. I don't know that there were more than one. I just know . . . Tina is gone, Custis. She is gone."

"Do you know how?"

"What do you mean?"

"I mean did somebody break in an' grab her in the night? Did they snatch her into a passing carriage? How'd they take her?"

"I don't actually know that."

"All right. Slow an' easy, tell me what you do know. Like when did this happen?"

"It was . . . last night. Yesterday evening, that is. Just past dark. I was b-b-baking. In the kitchen. I was mixing bread dough to set for th-this morning. I was right in the middle of scalding the milk when I remembered I used the last of my yeast the night before. I cussed a little. Out loud. Tina overheard. She said she would run down to Iler's store and get some. She said I should go ahead with my dough and she would have the yeast here before I was done with it.

"She . . . she didn't come back and she didn't come back, and after an hour or so I was frantic. You can imagine."

"Yes, I can, Mae darlin'. What happened next?"

"I cleaned up. Rinsed off my hands and face was all. And threw a shawl over my housedress. I ran over to Iler's."

"Iler's," Longarm repeated. "That's the little market in the next street over, ain't it?"

"Yes. Mr. Iler is . . . he's a very nice man. We do a lot of our business with him. We get our meat there. Other things. Anyway, I went there. Mr. Iler said that, yes, Tina was there earlier. He said sh-sh-she bought ten cents worth of yeast. He said she l-l-looked at his fancy éclairs. When he asked if she wanted one, she said no. She left then."

"Did he see did she turn toward home when she left his shop?" Longarm asked.

"I didn't think to ask that. Should I?"

"No, no. You did fine. Did you tell anybody? Did you tell the constable, for instance?"

"No. I haven't wanted to leave the house."

"Did you tell any of your guests?"

"I don't think so."

"Have you received any notes? Any message from Tina or a ransom note from the kidnapper, anything at all like that?"

Mae shook her head. "Oh, God, Custis. I don't know what to do," she wailed.

"You told me, darlin'. That was the best thing t' do. You know I'm crazy about that little girl. You know I'll go to hunting her. *And* the son of a worthless bitch that took her."

"Find her for me, Custis. I'm begging you. Find my baby."

"I will, darlin'. I promise."

Longarm hoped that was not a hollow promise, but he deemed it important right now to give Mae some small glimmer of hope amid her agony.

He might well be proved a liar later, but he would worry about that when the time came.

In the meantime, he also wanted to hope, difficult though that was.

The ugly truth, which he would not dream of sharing with the child's mother, was that there was damned little room for hope here.

Mae Washburn was not a wealthy woman. Someone bent on kidnap for ransom would likely take the child of a wealthy family. God knows there was plenty of money in Colorado City, and even more of it just four miles away in Colorado Springs. Besides, no ransom note had been delivered, and more than enough time had passed since Tina's disappearance for a kidnapper to hire a kid to deliver a note and then slink back into the shadows.

What Longarm feared, but hoped Mae had not thought about, was that Tina was budding into a young woman. Her hips and breasts were beginning to swell.

Any male who had reached puberty would be very much aware of that fact, and while Tina was not yet a beauty, perhaps never would be, she was tender and innocent and vulnerable.

There were some men who were attracted to that very innocence. Attracted enough to rape and then, once they were sated, to kill so their victim could not tell anyone.

Longarm checked his watch. Tina had been missing for—

"What time was this last night?"

"About ten."

Seventeen hours then, more or less. Shit!

Longarm turned Mae to face him and took both her hands in his. Very calmly, he continued questioning her. What was Tina wearing? How was her hair fixed? What sort of shoes did she have on? Was she carrying any money?

"Be patient with me, darlin'," he told Mae. "We can't

know yet what information is gonna be important, so I need t' know as much as you can tell me. Any detail. Everything you can think of, even silly stuff that couldn't be important. Tell me, please."

Chapter 12

Longarm was icy calm, his movements stiff with iron control. Rage would serve no purpose now. The time for that would come, though. Later. When he found the person or persons who had taken the child. That would be the time to unleash his fury.

Now he went down to the horses he had tied in front of Mae's house. He unstrapped the cinches on them and dumped the saddles unheeded on the ground, rifles and all, then buckled his own old McClellan onto the brown. The military-style saddle was an uncomfortable son of a bitch for the rider, but easy on the horse. That was important to the army. It was important as well to a vengeful Custis Long.

Longarm shoved his own trusted Winchester into the scabbard dangling from the McClellan, and threw his saddlebags over the brown's broad rump.

Leading both horses, he walked around the corner to the block where Iler's store was located. He did not immediately go there, however. First, he wanted to talk with the neighboring merchants. Iler could wait.

The first problem, the way Longarm saw it, was to figure

out if Tina was simply a convenient target of opportunity for some horny drunk or if she was deliberately targeted.

He quite frankly was not sure which of those he would prefer to learn.

Someone who snatched her on the spur of the moment might well rape the girl and then fear discovery afterward. He might choose to kill her once he sobered up and realized that he faced a hangman's noose if Tina fingered him to Colorado City Town Marshal Tom Eason. Or worse, to a mob of outraged citizens. All the swells who lived in the area were over in Colorado Springs. The Colorado City residents were more rough-and-tumble. They could form a hanging party in a heartbeat.

If she had been taken by someone like that, the girl probably was dead by now and her body hidden.

On the other hand, someone who was attracted to Tina in particular, someone, for instance, who'd stalked her and her alone, would likely want to keep her alive. For what ugly purposes only he could understand, but at least in that case she might well still be alive, serving that purpose.

And in that case, Longarm would have to be very careful how he approached the kidnapper lest he spook the sonuvabitch into getting rid of his victim.

That sort of thing happened. It was every lawman's fear.

Longarm flipped his wallet open to display his badge and began questioning the storekeepers in the vicinity of Iler's Market.

Chapter 13

"That's right. A tall, skinny drink o' water with reddish blond whiskers worn full, bib overalls, an' dirty red flannel longjohns but no proper shirt. Might've been in this neighborhood sometime over the past few days," Longarm said.

"Sure, I remember seeing that boy. I recall thinking at the time that he looked out of place around here. If you know what I mean."

"I'm not sure that I do. Please tell me."

"I just . . . this is a town. Workingman's town to be sure, but it's a town. This boy looked like he belonged on a farm, him and his floppy-brim straw hat and filthy dirty bare feet. Those longjohns weren't none too clean neither. I seen him standing around in the alley over there. Didn't look like he was up to any harm or I would've said something to the constable, but I seen him, sure enough. What did he do anyhow?"

"I don't know that he did anything, but pretty much everybody agrees he seemed out of place here."

"I'm not the only person that seen him then," the fellow suggested.

"No, sir, you're not."

In point of fact, this was the second of Mae Washburn's neighbors who reported seeing the same barefoot young man hanging around in the vicinity of Washburn House. No one exactly claimed that he was watching Tina. But no one knew any other reason for him to be there either.

In addition to these folks who lived close by Mae and Tina, three merchants and Ernest Iler all reported, in greater or lesser detail, having seen the same young man lurking in or near the alleys. Apparently, he had been there for at least three days and possibly longer. One woman who lived across the street from the Washburn House reported seeing him there every Sunday for the past two months, but Longarm noticed that she seemed to have difficulty with her vision. When he spoke with her, she squinted and kept shading her eyes, and he was standing face-to-face with her at the time. He was quite frankly skeptical of her claim to have seen the fellow at a distance. He doubted she could see the type on the pages of a book lying in her own lap.

He did accept the claims by the others, however.

This farm boy might—or might not—have been stalking Tina.

Tina might—or might not—have gone with him willingly.

It occurred to him that a young girl of Tina's tender age might think it romantic to be swept away by a handsome young man. Or by a pimple-faced youth if she could not find a handsome one.

Either way, whether she was kidnapped or ran away, Longarm had already promised Mae he would find her and return her. Tina and her mother could work out the details from that point on.

But God, he hoped the child was unharmed.

•   •   •

It was long after dark now, and very few lights could be seen behind the shades in the neighborhood. Even Iler's was closed for the evening.

Longarm could not shatter Mae's hopes by going back to her house. There was no way the distraught mother could understand that most times a manhunt is far from being the hell-for-leather chase that folks seemed to assume. First, a man had to find a direction to charge off toward. And oftimes, that can be a slow and frustrating process.

Better to be slow moving in the right direction, though, than fast in the wrong one. Billy Vail taught Longarm that long years ago. It was still true.

With a sigh of regret and a passing thought about the comforts to be found at Washburn House, Longarm mounted the brown horse and, leading the black, rode slowly down to Fountain Creek. There was a hobos' camp there where a man could generally cadge a potato hot out of the coals, especially if he had a pint to share in exchange for it.

Longarm had slept worse. And would again, he was sure.

"Pick it up, horse. Let's get some sleep before daybreak, shall we?"

The brown flicked its ears and tossed its head. Obviously by coincidence, Longarm thought.

Chapter 14

Longarm was waiting when the barbershop opened at seven. Past experience had shown that rich folks, such as the people who lived across the creek in Colorado Springs, are more willing to talk with someone if he is shaved and tidy than with a scruffy and unkempt examiner, even if he does carry the authority of a badge.

He got his shave, bought a new celluloid shirt collar that was crisp and white, and went back to questioning everyone he saw.

He got lucky when he talked to the driver on one of the town's streetcars.

"Sure, I saw him. Yesterday morning early, it was. Lanky kid driving a farm wagon. Right here in the city. That sort of rattletrap outfit might be all right down in Fountain or over in Colorado City where the working folks live, but it's sure as hell frowned on here. I even told Constable Wagner about it. Figured he might want to clue the young fella in before he got in trouble. Or caused some."

"D'you know if Wagner spoke with the young man?"

The driver shook his head. He checked his horses when they started to move forward, then glanced over his shoulder toward the two passengers in his car. They, too, were becoming impatient with this unscheduled stop. "I wouldn't know." The man picked up his driving lines, and was obviously about to put the car in motion again.

"One more thing," Longarm said. "Was this fellow alone?"

"Yes. Now you got to excuse me. I got to move along."

Longarm wheeled his mount along beside the streetcar tracks long enough to ask, "Where can I find Wagner?"

"Try the café. The one over close to the post office," the streetcar driver called over the rumble of the wheels.

There were two town constables having a mid-morning break when Longarm found the café, the two noticeable in their dark blue uniform coats and linen-covered helmets that aped the British bobby style. Someone obviously thought this was the up-to-date thing to do. Longarm just thought it looked silly. He pulled out a chair at their table and helped himself to a seat.

"Who the hell are you?" one of them demanded.

"I'm looking for Constable Wagner."

"Fine, but if you don't identify yourself, we'll run you in for vagrancy. Now I will ask this one more time and only one. Who are you?"

Longarm's frustrations boiled over. Before he had time to think about it, his Colt was out, the hard cold muzzle poking the constable in the man's left nostril.

Very slowly and distinctly, he said, "I am Deputy United States Marshal Custis Long, and I do not have either the time or the inclination to take any shit from the likes o' you. Now I asked you a civil question an' I will ask it again one more time and only one, as you so nicely put it. Where can I find a constable named Wagner?"

The second of the two at the table stammered, "Jesus, m-mister, put that thing away. I-I'm Wagner."

Longarm scowled. And shoved the .44 back into his holster. "Sorry. I'm in a hurry. Looking for a kidnapper an' I don't have any time to waste."

"A kidnapper. That's bad."

"Damn right it is. Now what I'm looking for is a fellow, might be you talked to him yesterday morning." Longarm repeated what he had been told about Tina's kidnapper.

"Sure, I remember him. Said his name was Teddy something-or-other, I disremember exactly what. He was driving this beat-up old farm wagon behind a pair of gray cobs. He was hauling some pigs, I think."

"Pigs?"

"I think so. That's what it sounded like anyhow."

"Sounded. You didn't see?"

"Couldn't. The wagon bed was covered with a tarp that was laced down snug. But the man said pigs, and I could hear them thumping and banging on the sides of the wagon and squealing."

"Dammit, man, those 'pigs' that you heard could've been a young girl who was tied and gagged back there."

"Well, the fellow said pigs and I heard pigs. I had no reason to think otherwise."

Longarm sighed. "No, I suppose not. Did he say where he was going?"

"East was all he told me. Said he was trying to go east. I told him that him and his wagon weren't welcome on the city streets. I told him to swing south, down Fountain way, that it would be all right for him to travel there."

"Did he?"

"Far as I know he did."

"As I recall, there isn't a whole hell of a lot out east of here," Longarm mused.

Constable Wagner said, "I wouldn't know. I'm from Boston myself. Just came here for the job."

Longarm grunted. Then rose. "Thanks for your help, fellas."

"Good luck, Marshal."

He headed for the door at a brisk walk. East, the man said. East it would be.

Chapter 15

Longarm pushed hard once he cleared the last of the plot markers laid out by the developers of the fancy young town. He was making up time at a good rate, moving far faster than a rickety farm wagon could travel. Even so, he was slowed by the need to stop at every house and hovel he spotted to make sure he was still following this Teddy something-or-other who had Tina Washburn in the bed of that rig.

Toward evening, Longarm figured he was still a good day and a half behind Teddy and Tina. The good news was that indeed he was behind them.

Teddy's course had veered a little north from the due-east path he'd initially followed. Had Longarm simply set out riding hell-for-leather eastward, by nightfall he would have been miles south of the wagon, that gap increasing the farther he rode.

As the daylight faded behind him, the sun long since having disappeared behind the Front Range mountains, Longarm spotted the smoke from a chimney a mile or so ahead. He rode toward it, to a crudely built sod house.

It was an impoverished homesteader's outfit and a poor one even by that standard. A few chickens hunkered down inside homemade cages, and a single cow and calf occupied a pen beside the soddy. A skinny mule grazed nearby. A small dog came yapping at the black's heels when Longarm approached. He drew rein in the bare patch that passed for a yard.

"Hello the house. Is anybody home?"

The beef hide that was hung over the doorway was pushed back a few inches, and Longarm could see someone peeping out. An eye. And the barrel of some sort of firearm.

"I'm friendly," he called. "Just lookin' for information an' maybe a meal if I could buy one off you. I'll pay cash money."

"Who are you?" It was a woman's voice, which perhaps explained the caution.

Longarm identified himself, and the woman stepped out into the open. She was tall and wiry, with steel gray hair and skin like leather. If she had a figure under her drab housedress, he could not determine what it might look like.

He could see quite plainly, however, that she was holding a shotgun, an old-fashioned muzzle loader. It was not cocked.

"Cash money, you said?"

"I did," he affirmed.

"How much?"

"A dollar." That was four times what a normal meal should cost, but she looked like she could use it.

"I got no grain for those horses."

"Hay would do."

"That would cost you extra."

"Another dollar for the horses then."

"Two dollars? Sure enough?"

"Sure enough."

"Step down and come inside. I'll have your supper ready by the time you're done tending your animals."

There was no pump in the yard, but there was a shallow well. Longarm drew water for the horses and then another bucket so he could wash himself a little. Rinse himself was more like it, since the lady of the manor did not offer soap. Plain water would do.

When he was done, he approached the soddy. "Ma'am? May I come in?"

"Come ahead."

He pushed the stiff beef hide aside, ducked his head to clear the deadwood that had been used as a lintel, and entered the sod house.

It was small. And then some. Room enough to turn around but not much more.

There was a rusty sheepherder's collapsible stove to one side, a blanket-covered cot on the other, and a tiny table, little more than a tall stool, in the middle. A three-legged milking stool sat beside the table. The only light came from the open door of the little stove, which seemed to be fired with dried cow and mule dung. A homemade basket of dry turds sat on the dirt floor close to the stove.

The table held a bowl of something that looked like milled oat porridge and a tin cup. The lady's beverage of choice seemed to be water.

Longarm had seen poor in his time. This woman could win a prize for it.

He dug into his pocket and found a gold quarter eagle.

"I don't have change for that," the lady informed him.

"Maybe that could cover breakfast, too," he suggested. The truth was that he had two silver dollars and probably that much again in smaller change. His use of the quarter eagle was deliberate.

63

"Sit then. Eat."

"Thank you, ma'am."

The porridge was bland to the point of being tasteless, and there was no milk to go with it nor any sugar. Still, it was warm and it filled the hollow spot in his belly. It would do. He ate quickly, then stood. "Thank you," he said again, and headed toward the doorway.

"You should lay your blankets inside here. Push the table back and lay out your bed there," the woman said. Longarm gave her a questioning look and she added, "There's likely to be a heavy dew tonight. You'll get wet and chilled if you sleep outdoors."

"Thanks for the warning." He wondered just what in hell this lady was up to. The air here on the grassy plains was dry. There would be no dew tonight. There almost never was.

He laid out his bed where she said.

Chapter 16

Longarm woke instantly and completely, with no lagging grogginess to dull his senses. He always slept light when he was among strangers, and he was not at all certain of this lady's intentions.

He heard the ropes under her mattress creak, and his right hand beneath his blanket shifted to the grips of the Colt that rarely left his side. He lay quiet, eyes closed but ears closely tuned, while the lady stood and moved to the stove.

A brief wash of light filled the tiny soddy when she opened the firebox and added some fuel. No harm in that. Longarm relaxed just a little.

He heard the very faint shuffle of her feet on the packed earth floor as she approached his bed.

Then he heard the even fainter rustle of falling cloth.

He opened his eyes to find her standing naked over him.

The woman was thin to the point of being scrawny. Her rib cage stood out plain beneath her skin, and her pelvic bones were as sharp as ax heads.

Her pubic hair was a scant dusting of gray over a protruding mound with a gaping slash of red on it. Her tits were flaccid bags of skin tipped with large, purple nipples. If there had ever been any sort of flesh inside those bags, it had all long since dried up and disappeared.

Seen naked, she looked even older than when she was clothed. Almost feeble in appearance.

She was bold enough to go after what she wanted, though. When she saw Longarm's open eyes peering up at her, she dropped to her knees and bent over him. The wrinkled bags of skin on her chest hung forward, giving him a look at what her tits must have been like when she was young and they were perky.

She pulled his blanket back and rocked back on her heels, hunkering there and admiring the size of him.

Longarm had not intended it—really he had not—but under her scrutiny, his cock began to engorge and grow. In less than a minute, it was standing upright.

The woman reached down with one hand and took his balls onto her fingertips. She lifted them as if trying to judge their weight, then slid that hand up onto the base of his shaft. Her fingers curled around his cock and tightened, then quickly released. She smiled.

Longarm lay where he was. Watching. Silent.

The woman bent low again. Her lips, thin and lined with age, parted and her tongue flicked in and out several times.

Then she took him into her mouth.

This was a woman who knew how to suck a cock. She held him inside her mouth and ran her tongue around and around the head of his dick. Longarm thought he was going to get off then and there.

She seemed to sense how very close he was, and she quickly backed off, letting his dick slide out of the warmth in her mouth into the chill of the air.

The fingers that had been on his balls went back down

there, then lower still. She found the tightly puckered rose-bud that was his asshole and circled it with one fingertip. At the same time, she began licking and very gently suckling Longarm's left nipple.

He groaned, the sound eliciting a slight smile on the woman's face.

She sat up and rocked back on her heels again, her knees splayed wide so that he could see the dark red slash that was her pussy. She spat onto the fingertips of one hand and applied the spittle to her pussy, then straddled Longarm's waist.

Using one hand to brace herself and the other to guide his cock, she pressed her hips down and forward.

He felt her flesh part for his entry. Then he was enveloped by the heat of her body.

Longarm started to lift his hips to her, but she pressed the palm of her hand down on his belly and shook her head. She wanted him to lie still. She wanted to do this. He lay back, still inside her, and closed his eyes, giving himself to the sensations.

She began to rotate her hips. Slowly. Gently. Then faster. Much faster. Hard. Almost brutal.

She speared herself on his sword.

Stiffened.

Cried aloud.

Longarm felt the contractions of her flesh tight around his, and the hot, sweet sap began to rise in him until he could contain it no longer. His seed burst out into her, and he moaned loud and long.

The woman shuddered a few times. Then she stood, letting him flop free.

Matter-of-factly, as if nothing had happened beyond feeding the fire, she gathered up her discarded nightdress and slipped it over her head. She lay back down on her cot, and within seconds appeared to be asleep.

Not a word had been spoken. But then none was necessary.

Longarm let go of his revolver, which remained forgotten in his hand. He pulled the blanket over him again, closed his eyes, and soon enough he, too, was once more sleeping.

Chapter 17

Longarm was an hour down the road the next morning before he realized that he had no idea what the woman's name was or why she was living alone so far from any family or neighbors. Not that it was any of his business.

This was empty country, gently rolling grassland that used to feed buffalo by the tens of thousands. The buffalo were gone but the grass remained, grass that was as nourishing for long-horned beeves as it had been for the woollies. There were few ranches where he could ask about Teddy and the tarp-covered farm wagon, but he did occasionally see another human, most generally a waddie or two tending to the needs of free-ranging cattle.

About mid-morning, he spotted the slowly moving blades of a windmill fan. As he came closer, he could see the tower. A man was crouching on the platform, and there was another fellow on the ground. Two horses were tied beside the wooden stock tank that the windmill fed.

"Howdy," Longarm said when he was near. "Mind if I water my animals here?"

"Help yourself, mister."

Longarm stepped down. He transferred his saddle onto

the black, then led both horses over to the tank where they could drink. "Thanks." He peered up at the wiry fellow who was on the tower. "Problems?"

"No problems," the cowpuncher at ground level said. "Just oiling the gears and packing the sucker with grease. Routine stuff."

"I suppose you boys would get a good look at everything for miles around," Longarm said.

"I suppose we would. Is there something in particular you have in mind, mister?"

"Matter o' fact there is. I'm looking for a fellow, redheaded man with a beard, driving a farm wagon. I'm trying to catch up with him. Has he passed this way?"

"Nope. Not while we been here."

"Oh, hell, Pete, don't be so closemouthed all the time," the man on the tower called down. "The man you want didn't come by here exactly, but yesterday afternoon we saw just such a rig camped by Antelope Creek. That's about, oh, eighteen or twenty miles east from here and a little bit north. Said he stopped early because he needed to mend some harness." The waddie snorted. "Wasn't harness he had on his mind, I'd say. It was that girl that was with him."

"What did the girl look like?"

"Hell, I dunno. We never got a good look at her. She was setting by the fire, all hunched over with a blanket draped over her Injun fashion. But it was a girl all right. You could tell that by the way this redheaded fellow kept himself in between her and us. He didn't want us coming close to her. Not that we would have, mind you, but he seemed touchy about it."

"Antelope Creek you say."

"I dunno what it would be on a map, but that's what we call it hereabouts."

"East by a little bit north."

"That's right."

"Bobby, you got a big mouth on you. What if that fella don't want to be found."

"You oughtn't be so suspicious of everything, Pete."

"And you oughtn't to talk so much."

"Gentlemen, I didn't mean to cause a problem here, and I thank you for the water. Now if you'll excuse me, I'll be on my way." Longarm pulled his cinch strap snug, then stepped into the saddle.

He was finding that the black horse was a good mount out here away from the rocky mountain terrain. It had an easy gait and good stamina. Between it and the brown, he was able to cover ground at a good clip. The only problem was knowing where to find Teddy. And Tina.

She was still alive, though. She almost had to have been the girl under the blanket. She was still alive and that was the important thing.

"Take it easy, gentlemen," Longarm said. He touched a finger to his hat brim and a spur to the black.

Chapter 18

"Sure, I seen those two. Redheaded fella driving a old wagon an' a quiet little gal on the seat beside him. Not very friendly either one of them, but I seen them all right. Driving east."

"Did they say where they were going?"

The sheepherder shrugged. "Something about going to a wedding. I wished I coulda gone along, but sheep folks ain't generally welcome at most shindigs. If I coulda, though, I woulda turned and gone right along with 'em."

"That was today?" Longarm asked.

"Hell, that was less'n two hours ago. Maybe closer to one."

Longarm stood in his stirrups and swiveled around toward the west. The sun was already below where he judged the distant horizon to be and the shadows were deep. It likely would be full dark in twenty or thirty minutes. But he was only two hours behind Tina now. Perhaps less.

"Due east, you say."

"That's right," the sheepherder said. "Or maybe a little south of east."

"He didn't say where this wedding would take place?"

The man dug a fingernail into the depths of his beard

and scratched his neck, then shook his head. "Didn't say exactly, but there's a . . . well, I wouldn't call it a town nor even a village; it ain't that big . . . but there's a sort of community to the south a piece. Just a store an' a little church an' a couple houses. The storekeeper is the preacher, too, you see. Him and his family are the ones that live there. Could be the place they figure to hold the wedding. That's just a guess, of course."

"South, you say."

"That's right. If you go straight east, you'll strike the National Road. You can't miss it. Just turn right there an' it'll take you down to that community."

"The Ogalalla National Road, you mean?"

"That's it. I couldn't recall the name. I'd follow it my own self but for two things. The cattlemen frown on having sheep around anyway, and all them beeves have the grass pounded clean away by so many of them trampling it underfoot."

That made sense. The Ogalalla was the government's answer to the needs of the cattlemen after quarantines were imposed in east and central Kansas. That shut down the cow towns. The Ogalalla National Road swung well west of the settled parts of Kansas and ran up the Kansas-Colorado line to reach the rich, new grazing lands in Wyoming, Nebraska, and Montana.

If he was this close to the Ogalalla, he must be in Kansas now or soon would be.

"Two hours, eh?"

"Less prob'ly."

Longarm thanked the man, switched his saddle again, and mounted. He set off to the east at a steady canter.

The road was plain enough even by the faint light from the stars wheeling bright overhead.

It was not, however, something an Eastern visitor might recognize as a road. There was no narrow, graded surface. Certainly, there was no long stretch of gravel.

Instead, this was a bare, beaten path across an already sere and dusty grassland. The grass had been trampled into dust in a north-south swath that was a good quarter mile wide. Cattle by the tens of thousands had been driven up this barely marked road, some destined for the transcontinental railroad, most to stock the huge ranches that were still being established on the great northern grasslands now that the threat of Indian depredations seemed to have lessened.

Longarm drew rein at the edge of the road and hesitated for a moment.

There might be a wedding planned at the settlement to the south. Or there might not be. Whatever he did would be a gamble.

"Fuck it," he said aloud.

He kneed the brown into a trot and swung south.

Chapter 19

A store, a church, and a couple houses. That is how that sheepherder described the settlement along the Ogalalla. Despite knowing that and being on the lookout for it, Longarm almost rode right past. Probably would have had he not spotted a candle's glow in a window.

The community was set a half mile or so off the road—the better to avoid noise and dust and errant longhorns most likely—in the bottom of a shallow swale. A few undernourished cottonwoods provided scant shelter from wind, sun, or snow.

Longarm reined off the trail and approached the houses. He sat in his saddle for several minutes expecting someone to notice his presence so he could make the obligatory polite request that he get down. No one did, so eventually he stepped down without permission.

He tied his mounts outside the building he guessed was the store, although it could as easily have been the church. There were no signs or markings, at least none that he could see in the dark. There was, however, a candle guttering behind a pane of flyspecked glass.

A knock on that door brought no response. He was rapping on the door that he guessed led into the building when he heard the creak of hinges. Yellow light spilled out of a doorway at one of the houses and a barefoot man wearing a nightshirt and sleeping cap stepped outside holding a lamp high.

"Hello? Is someone there?"

"Yes, sir. Over here."

"I'm sorry, son. The store is closed. Come again in the morning."

"I'm not here t' shop, friend. Are you the headman around here?"

"That is a term I do not know, but I am the pastor if that is what you mean, and the storekeeper as well. My name is Barnaby Adams."

Longarm left the horses where they were and walked over to the man. He introduced himself and said, "I was told there was s'posed to be a wedding around here somewheres, Mr. Adams. Figured it must be here. So where's all the folks from the marryin'?"

The preacher shook his head. "There has been no wedding ceremony performed here. Not ever, although certainly I would be honored to preside over such."

"How's about a redheaded fella named Ted drivin' a wagon? Has a young girl with him. Have you seen them?"

"I'm sorry, but no. I have not."

"Seen them drive by this evening maybe, headed south? Could they've gone by without you noticing them?"

"No, I generally keep an eye on the road. I know what moves along it. I saw a group of men with a pack string come past just before sunset. They were northbound. They tried to buy whiskey from me. I do not deal in alcoholic spirits. When I told them that, they made some . . . well . . .

some very crude comments. Then they left. Frankly, I was glad to see them go. I was afraid they might want to spend the night nearby. But I saw no wagon driving in either direction. Have not since, oh, yesterday morning, I believe it was. That wagon was traveling south. Could this have been the party you mean?"

"Shit!" Longarm grumbled. The epithet earned him a sharp look from Preacher Adams.

"Sorry," he quickly said. But . . . shit!

He had ridden miles out of his way and worn down his horses, and all for nothing.

Now he had to turn around and head north.

The good thing there was that Teddy did not know he was being pursued. He was not moving fast to begin with, apparently stopping overnight, taking his time in camp, and doing whatever the hell he did with Tina. Longarm did not want to think about that. Better not to.

The bad thing was that the horses needed rest, water, and feed. In that order.

"Pastor, would it be all right if I camp here for the night?"

"Of course." The man pointed behind the church building. "There is a good place over there where many before you have slept and a well where you can draw water."

"Any charge for the water, pastor?"

"It is not my water, son. It is God's and you are free to use it for the nourishment of your body and those of your animals." He winked. "Morning coffee, on the other hand, will be five cents if you would care for some."

Longarm laughed. "Thank you, pastor. I'll keep that in mind." Not that he actually expected to still be here come morning. He suspected by the time this gentleman woke up, Longarm would be a good many miles to the north and moving as fast as he thought his horses could manage.

"Good night, sir, and thank you again."

"Good night, young man. God bless."

Longarm found the well Preacher Adams mentioned and drew fresh water for the horses. He wanted to get them bedded down soon so they would be as rested and ready in the morning as was possible.

Tomorrow, tomorrow at the latest, he should catch up with Teddy.

Chapter 20

Longarm caught up with Teddy in the cool of the morning just as the rising sun was creating a red crescent glow to the east. He had rested only a few hours, then saddled his weary horses and pointed them north.

Now he finally caught up with Teddy.

Teddy lay huddled beside his wagon, slumped low against a wheel, blood covering his face and his hands, which were clutching with desperate strength against his belly.

The wagon tarp was pulled back and the wagon was empty, the big horses that had been pulling it hobbled and placidly grazing nearby.

Longarm swung off the black horse and tied both of his animals to a wheel on the opposite side from where Teddy lay. He walked around to the wounded man and knelt at his side.

Teddy was as had been described. A little smaller than Longarm expected perhaps, but there was no doubt that this was the kidnapper.

"Teddy? Open your eyes, Teddy. Can you talk? Tell me what happened here."

Teddy's eyes fluttered and he took a long, shallow breath. Even that seemed to send spasms of pain through him. A fresh spill of blood flowed through his fingers.

Up close like this, Longarm could see that Teddy's belly had been sliced open. Gray coils of gut showed behind the hands that tried to hold him together. Whoever did this did it out of pure meanness. It would have been merciful to put a bullet in his brain.

Longarm fetched his canteen and pulled Teddy's neckerchief off. He wet it and used it to bathe Teddy's face. Teddy opened his eyes.

"I'm a deputy United States marshal," Longarm said soothingly. "I'm lookin' for Tina Washburn. I b'lieve she was, um, riding with you."

Teddy licked his lips, tried to speak, had to pause and try again. "Tina. We was . . . gonna get . . . get married. We was . . . going to my . . . folks' place. Over near . . . Leavenworth. Last night. Some men. They . . . come on our camp. They said . . . ugly things. They wanted to . . . to buy Tina." Teddy's eyes squeezed closed and tears began to trickle out of them. "I . . . love her. Tried to stop . . . stop them. They did . . . this to me. Mister, find her. Help her. I never would've hurt her. Never. Now . . . those men."

"Tell me about the men, Teddy."

"They was . . . five of them. Packhorses. Buff'lo hunters maybe. Or fur trappers. They was . . . five of them. Tried to stop them. I swear to God I tried to stop them. Mister, find Tina. Get her clear from those . . . men. Please."

Teddy did not ask help for himself, Longarm noted. He only asked that Tina be saved. Perhaps he did love her, at least in his own way.

"You know what's in store for you, don't you, Teddy?"

"I know, mister. I'd stop the hurting, but they come on

me so quick I couldn't get to my pistol. Could you . . . could you hand it to me. Please?"

"Where is it, Teddy?"

"Front of . . . of the wagon. In a nose bag. Under the seat. And one other thing, mister. Would you . . . turn my pap's horses loose. They'll find their way back to him if you do that."

"Sure, Teddy. I'll do that for you."

Longarm walked to the front of the wagon. He climbed up on the wheel and peered beneath the seat. A pair of canvas nose bags were wadded up and stuck in a corner of the driving box. An old Starr cap-and-ball revolver, the bluing long since worn away, was in one of the bags. Longarm checked the loads, then handed the pistol to Teddy.

Before he had time to walk out to the farm horses to unfasten their hobbles, he heard a muffled explosion.

The old gun still worked, it seemed.

Chapter 21

Five men. Moving north on the National Road. Longarm threw the stub of a cheroot down and angrily ground it underfoot.

He was frustrated. His horses were weary. Hell, he was bone tired himself. And from here the nameless, faceless men could go . . . anywhere. All of the northern plains lay open to them from here.

And they had Tina. Damn them, they had Tina.

Longarm did not know, and at this point did not really care, whether Tina had willingly gone with Teddy-something. She may have chosen to go. She may have been kidnapped. That was not really important now.

Now his concern had to be getting her away from the five men who had stolen her.

There was no question of her willingness to go with the five, whatever she may or may not have thought about Teddy and his marriage plans. Now she damn sure had been kidnapped. It was his job to get her back again.

Poor, dumb Teddy.

Longarm had no time to waste digging holes in the ground. Someone else would have to bury Teddy. Lordy, he just hoped someone came by who knew who the kid was so his family could be told.

Perhaps someone could follow the horses back to find him and the wagon. In the meantime, Longarm had miles to cover.

He freed the tarpaulin from the tie-down hooks on the wagon box and hauled the stiff, grease-stained tarp off the wagon to cover Teddy's body. He weighted the edges with trace chain so the wind would not blow the cover off, then went around to where he had left his horses.

Longarm switched his saddle yet again and swung onto the brown.

He drew rein on top of a low hogback. He was not sure, but thought he saw a wisp of white smoke rising out of a line of trees a mile or so ahead. He had not seen any sign of humans since he left Teddy and that farm wagon several hours earlier.

Two miles back, he had crossed a dry creek bed, the relatively moist earth a tangle of chokecherry and crack willow. Ahead, he could see trees. Actual trees. Those were rare in western Kansas. Unless this was eastern Colorado. Or southern Nebraska. Hell, it could be any one of them. Maybe someplace else for all he knew.

What he was sure of was that he was tired enough to fall off this horse, and if he did fall off he would likely just lie there and start to snore. He touched his spurs to the beast's flanks and set it into a rocking-chair canter toward that smoke.

The smoke, he figured, meant one of two things. Trouble or food. His mood was such that he would almost welcome some trouble, and his belly was empty enough that he for damned sure would welcome food.

As he came nearer, he could see that an intermittent creek lay ahead, the watercourse mostly dry now, but with some deep pools that likely would remain until rains over in Colorado filled the stream.

A narrow road ran east-west on that side of the creek also, and the trees sheltered a sturdy building—part split log and part cut sod—and a large corral that held a dozen or more heavy horses. Haying equipment was parked beneath an open-sided shed, and there was a tarp-covered haystack close to the corral.

As Longarm approached, he could hear the ring of steel on steel. Someone doing some blacksmithing perhaps. Of much more interest to him, he could smell the tantalizing aroma of wood smoke and frying meat.

At the moment, he would sign over his pension—assuming he might live long enough to someday get one—in exchange for a bowl of pottage. Or a pork chop.

He guided his two horses down into the creek bed and across the hard, gravel bottom, then up the other side. The smell of cooking meat was even stronger there, and he was drawn to it as surely as a fly will find honey.

There was a covered front porch along the front of the building. Wooden benches were lined up against the wall, enough to accommodate maybe sixteen people at a time, never mind that there was no bunkhouse to suggest that this was somebody's ranch headquarters.

And there were no signs posted indicating that this was a store, nor any hitching rail close by the building.

Longarm grunted. He did not know where he was, but he guessed he had wandered into some stage line's relay station.

He dismounted, his joints feeling the abuse he had put on them over the past few days, and tied the horses to a corral rail.

Chapter 22

The gent with the bushy sidewhiskers gave Longarm a long, skeptical examination before he answered the question. "You're in Kansas, mister. Colorado is a few miles over that way." He jerked a thumb by way of giving direction.

"Nebraska is still a pretty good piece up that way." A finger pointed north. "Do you want us to make you out a map?"

"I could stand for you t' quit being a smart-ass," Longarm said. "I'm too tired for that kinda shit right now."

"Now isn't that just a brass-bound pity," Sidewhiskers sneered.

"Look, mister, I didn't come in here for a argument. I'm tired, I'm hungry, an' I need your help, not your sass. Now would that be all right?"

"Both of you climb down off your high horses," the smaller of the two station keepers interjected. That one was slightly built and balding. His mouthy friend was a head taller. Neither of them was big on shaving.

"I'm not lookin' for no trouble," Longarm said. "I just come here t' get a meal an' maybe some information. Quick as I do that, I'll catch up a couple o' those horses out there an' be on my way."

"What horses would those be, mister, the ones you expect to catch up and ride away on?"

"I notice in your corral there's some that your people bought from the army. They got cavalry troop markings on their forequarters. That means they're trained to saddle. I'm gonna have to swap you my two horses for a pair o' yours."

"Like hell you will," the smaller man snapped. "They belong to the Gardner and Feeley Express Company. What's more, you are not a passenger with the line. We aren't required to feed you. Now I would appreciate it if you would leave. Now!" He turned around and fumbled in a broom cupboard. He came out of it holding a single-barrel shotgun, probably something the two of them used to bring in meat for the pot.

Longarm ignored the shotgun—which might or might not be loaded to begin with—and flipped his wallet open to display his badge.

"What the hell is that?" the larger man demanded.

"Just what it looks like." Longarm introduced himself and added, "I'm chasing a gang of kidnappers. I'm thinking they might've come through this way. Five men, dragging a little girl with them. Got some pack animals, I'm told, though I don't know how many or what sort."

"Kidnappers, you say?"

"That's right. The little girl's name is Tina. She's from Colorado City."

"Shit," the smaller man said.

"They were here?"

"I think it maybe was them. Real late last night, somebody came through. I couldn't see who they were or how many. They wanted to buy whiskey. We sell it, but only to passengers, and then only by the drink. We don't sell by the bottle."

"You turned them away?"

"That's right. The door was already closed and barred for the night. We didn't open it to them. I noticed this morning they stole some hay from us, but better that than serious trouble."

"The last fellow whose path they crossed wasn't as lucky as you boys," Longarm said. "They cut his belly open an' spilled his guts into his lap. You did right to keep them out. What about the girl? Did you see her? Was she all right?"

"I didn't see any girl. How about you, Titus?"

The taller fellow shook his head. "I didn't get a really good look at any of them."

"Fellas, I'm about to starve. I need t' get some food in me, an' I need to switch out them horses. I don't wanta be a hard-ass about this, but it's important."

"I'll say it's important," the shorter man agreed. He looked at his partner and said, "Go lead out horses for the man. Shiloh and Gettysburg, I think. They're the steadiest under saddle, and they're both good and rested."

"Shiloh and Gettysburg?" Longarm asked.

The fellow shrugged. "The boss, he's a veteran of the war. He names all the horses things like that. You don't have to worry about their names. Like you said yourself, they're both ex-cavalry. They'll do fine for you. Just don't put up with any shit off them, and they'll go good under saddle again."

Titus left, and the little fellow said, "Sit down. While

he's getting your mounts ready, I'll put a plate on the table for you. I'll fix up a poke for you to carry along, too, if you like."

"Make it stuff I can grab and chew on the run if you don't mind. I don't want t' waste no time about this. The quicker I get that child back to her mama the better."

"You said you're tired, Marshal. Would you like to lie down for a little rest before you go?"

"Like to? Friend, I'd kill for an uninterrupted hour o' sleep right now, but I ain't got time for such." Longarm managed a smile. "Hell, I'll sleep twice tonight t' make up for it."

"Yeah, that ought to do it." The little man, whose name Longarm never had heard, took the station operators' own dinner out of the skillet and piled it, all of it, onto a plate that he set before Longarm. "Eat this. It will put hair on your chest." He turned around and grabbed up a burlap sack that he began loading with food for Longarm to carry along with him—jerky and hardtack and other traveling goods that their stagecoach customers might ask for to comfort them along the way.

When Longarm had eaten and had the sack dangling from one hand, he shoved his other hand into his pocket. "How much do I owe you for all o' this, friend?"

"Owe? The hell you say. You don't owe us anything. I just hope you catch those bastards and get that child back to her mother."

"I'm in your debt, friend."

"It's a debt you can pay by getting your butt back in that saddle and finding the kid. Okay?"

"Okay. And . . . thanks." He knew of no stronger way to say it. He hoped these two way station operators understood that.

Longarm turned and headed out to where two horses stood waiting, one already carrying his saddle.

Funny, but he felt almost rested when he swung into the saddle this time.

Chapter 23

•

It was a town. It wasn't much of a town, but he supposed it should qualify as one. It had a main street with five businesses on it—a general mercantile, a smithy, a barber, a hardware, and a saloon—with a dozen or more small houses scattered nearby.

The most important feature from Longarm's point of view was that it was on a telegraph line. Poles and wire extended from the back of the mercantile into the distance toward the east.

There was no livery, but behind the general store there was a wagon park. Longarm left his horses there and walked stiff-legged, his eyes grainy and burning from fatigue, into the store.

He had been in the saddle for . . . he honestly could not work it out. Could not get his mind around it.

He remembered being on the lookout above South Park. That was where he picked up the horses left by the dead coach robber. Then down to Colorado City. East to Kansas. North to where he found Teddy-something. Then the stagecoach station. Then . . . what had it been? Another three days? He thought so.

Time and scenery blurred. He ate when he was hungry. When he ran out of food, he made do with water taken from the occasional stream that he crossed. He followed the National Road. Light turned to dark turned to light again. All he knew was that he had to find those men. He had to find Tina.

It was past noon when he reached this tiny prairie town that might or as easily might not survive. Communities like this popped up, briefly flourished until the newcomers learned the heartbreak of farming on the plains, and then as quickly died. They seemed almost as fragile as the mining camps that boomed and fizzled.

In the mountain gold camps or down here in the vast flatlands, it was easier to move on—to new opportunities, to newer and grander dreams—than it was to hang in when things got tough.

"Hello, friend. What can I do for you?" The storekeeper was a portly, smiling man in sleeve garters.

Longarm introduced himself and explained his problem. "Have you seen these men? Five of 'em and a little girl."

Lordy, he hoped Tina was still with them. They could well have murdered the child and abandoned her body or buried her somewhere. They could also have turned off to either side without him knowing.

The storekeeper shook his head. "I've had a man I didn't know come in and buy some foodstuffs. That would have been yesterday about this time of day. But he was alone and I saw no child with him."

Longarm sighed. "I think . . . I think what I need t' do is send wires out to whatever towns are around here. See if I can get a line on them that way. Otherwise, I could go larrupin' off in the wrong direction an' never catch up with them. You got a message pad an' pencil? I'll write something out an' ask you to distribute it for, oh, about fifty miles in any direction. Can you do that for me?"

The storekeeper was already reaching for a pad of paper when he answered, "Of course, Marshal. I just hope I can help."

Once the message was written down and passed across to the storekeeper, who doubled here as the town's telegrapher, the fellow said, "You know, Marshal, it will take a while, probably hours, for answers to come in from these. May I suggest that you go over to the house at the edge of town. The one in that direction"—he pointed—"with the blue shutters. It's sort of a secret, but Mrs. Collins there welcomes gentlemen to, um, visit. You could lie down there and catch some sleep. I'll come wake you if anyone thinks they've seen your kidnappers."

"I cannot tell you how fine I think your idea is, mister."

"Sam," he said. "My name is Sam Johnson. You can tell Mrs. Collins that I sent you."

"Thanks, Sam. You're a lifesaver."

Longarm turned away and stumbled out into the sunlight. He blinked and rubbed his burning eyes, spotted the house Sam Johnson described, and headed toward it.

Chapter 24

"Sam sent you? And you are a marshal? How exciting. Please come in. Oh, my. You look exhausted. Filthy, too. I hope you don't mind me saying that. I always try to say what is true. Now come inside." She smiled hugely. "Let me take care of you."

Amanda Collins turned out to be a slightly plump woman who looked like she belonged in a high-toned ladies' church social. Her hair was beginning to turn gray, and there were deep wrinkles around her eyes and at the corners of her mouth.

She stood perhaps five feet tall. If that. And she gave the impression that if she was not a mother, then she damn well ought to be. Longarm liked her immediately. More surprising, he trusted her. She managed to make him feel like he was coming home.

"Come inside now. I'll take you to your room."

The bedroom was small and stuffed full of furniture. So were the other rooms he passed through on the way there. Longarm got the idea that Mrs. Collins had moved here from a much larger—and much finer—house elsewhere.

In addition to a huge wardrobe, dresser, chest of drawers,

and double bed, a copper slipper tub was occupying the space at the foot of the bed. For some reason, it already held water.

"Now I want you to know, Marshal, that I am what is known as a grass widow. I have a husband. Somewhere. Assuming no one has had the good sense to kill him before now. My point is, I am not shocked by the sight of a naked gentleman. In fact, I rather like it."

While she spoke her fingers were busy working on his buttons. Longarm was so tired, he hardly noticed.

"Now you are not going to get into my nice clean sheets until you have a bath, Marshal. But don't you worry. I have hot water in the stove reservoir. I shall give you a nice warm bath. Sit down now while I get these boots off. Oh!" She held her nose and made a sour face, then laughed at her own joke when the boots came off his feet for the first time in days.

"I have some nice talcum powder that I can shake into these boots. It will help dry them and make them smell better, too. Take my hand. I wouldn't want you to lose your balance. Step into the tub now. Sit down. There, doesn't that feel good? I knew it would.

"Just lean back now and let me wash you. Here. This soap, I think. It doesn't smell too flowery for a gentleman. Does that feel good? I knew it would. When you wake up, I can give you a shave. My dearly departed husband . . . although exactly where he departed to I could not tell you . . . used to like for me to shave him. I can assure you I will do a good job. I probably won't nick you more than seven or eight times." She laughed again.

Between the warm water and Mrs. Collins's hands moving gently over his skin, Longarm was already half asleep. Her words came to him as if through a fog.

"Oh! Lovely," was her comment when she came to his crotch. He did not even get a hard-on when she washed and rinsed him there.

She bathed him thoroughly, then helped him stand and used a fluffy towel to dry him off.

"Into bed with you now, dear man. And don't worry. I'm not running off with these clothes. I do intend to wash them while you sleep, though. I'll hang your pistol on the bedpost. It's right here now, do you see? Here, let me plump that pillow for you and tuck you in."

Longarm presumed that she would do what she said. But he never felt her tuck the covers high under his chin.

He was asleep before the lady had time to do that.

Chapter 25

He came awake as gently as he fell asleep, slowly drifting up from the depths of slumber to a groggy awareness.

Before he was completely awake, while he still felt as if he were floating somewhere just slightly below the surface of consciousness, Longarm felt a pleasant warmth in his belly.

Gradually, he came to realize that it was not actually his belly that he was feeling but his lower midsection. Somewhere in his crotch.

The sensation localized itself and he was mildly, but quite pleasantly, surprised to discover that it was his cock that felt warm. Warm and . . . wet as well.

He had a hard-on, although he did not know why he should.

And it felt good. It felt—

He was being sucked. Very gently, but with a strong suction accompanied by the swirl of a tongue around and beneath the head of his cock. Whoever was doing this knew what she was about.

Come to think of it, who the hell *was* doing this?

Longarm's eyes popped open and he came fully awake to discover the top of Mrs. Collins's graying head bobbing up and down over his crotch, his pecker in her mouth and his balls cupped warm and cozy in the palm of her hand.

He yawned and stretched, the movement tipping her off that he had wakened. She stopped what she was doing and lifted her face a bit to free her tongue. "Good morning. Did you sleep well?" Her pleasant tone of voice was as normal as if she were greeting him on a public street. She smiled.

"Yeah, uh, I did. Thanks."

"I'm so glad. We shall have breakfast in a few minutes. Let me finish this first, please." Mrs. Collins smiled again, then dipped her head and opened her mouth to take him inside.

She did not stop again until she had his come in her throat. Then she clamped her lips shut lest she spill any while she picked up a damp washcloth that she had left nearby. She carefully wiped him off and patted his cock, then laid it gently down.

Only then did she swish his juices back and forth in her mouth and, smiling, swallow it all down.

She smacked her lips. "Tasty," she said.

She wriggled backward off the bed—she was fully dressed and in fact looked quite prim and proper now—and said, "I've washed your things but they are not quite dry. I do have some things that belonged to my husband. And, well, I have a few other articles of clothing in the house, too. I am sure I can find something to fit you. Something clean and dry. If you would not be too proud to accept them, that is."

"Anything that's good enough for me t' walk out in public," he said. "I ain't proud." That was not completely true. Longarm took great pride in some things. Neither his own appearance nor his personal dignity was among them, however. And he did not fancy the idea of pulling on wet clothes.

Mrs. Collins brought him a selection of shirts and trousers to try on, then said, "Wear whichever of them you like. While you are doing that, I shall go start your breakfast."

"What time is it anyhow?" he asked, peering toward the lowered window shade where there was a hint of strong sunlight behind it.

"About ten o'clock, I think."

"Shouldn't it be dark out at ten?"

She laughed. "Ten in the morning, dear man. You slept the clock around."

"What about . . . ?"

"He came by," she said, cutting him off. "Twice actually. He said to tell you he heard back from two of his wires, but the gentlemen in those towns say they have not seen the party you are looking for. He said there are two others he hasn't yet heard from."

Longarm yawned. "Can't believe I slept that long."

"You were exhausted."

"Maybe so, but that's no excuse. There's a young girl counting on me t' get her away from those animals."

"If dire things have happened to her, Marshal, it is already too late for you to save her from them. It will be a terrible shame if she has been raped, but it is something she can survive. If she is strong enough and if people let her put it behind her. Your job now is to find her and get her away from her captors."

"If she's still alive," Longarm said.

"Yes, and if not, then you must find the men and punish them. But, dear man, you have to be strong enough yourself to do this. Now try on those clothes while I go fix you some sausage and biscuits for breakfast. Would you like some greens to go with that?"

"Don't bother with the greens, but I sure have a taste for sausage gravy t' pour on my biscuits."

"Then gravy it shall be. Go on now. It will be on the table in ten minutes."

The plump little woman scurried out, and Longarm got busy sorting through the clothing she had brought in.

Chapter 26

Longarm felt better, a helluva lot better, when he walked outside Amanda Collins's house. He was clean and fed and rested, and if his clothes did not fit perfectly, they were clean and sturdy. His own things were still hanging on a clothesline behind the Collins house. If he had time, he would collect them later. If not, a few articles of clothing would be a small price to pay for a chance to get back on the trail of Tina's kidnappers.

"Hello, Sam," he greeted the storekeeper. "Any news?"

Johnson shook his head. "Nothing except those reports I already gave to Amanda. She gave them to you, I suppose?"

"She did. She also said you got some more yet t' come."

"That's right. Two more. I'm hoping to hear something today."

"I tell you what then. I'm gonna go over to that saloon I seen down the street. I'll ask there if they know anything. Might even have something t' warm my belly while it's handy."

"All right. If I hear anything, I'll come tell you."

"Thanks, Sam. You been a help an' I appreciate it."

Longarm first went back to the wagon park to check on

his horses and on the saddle he had left there. He threw a little hay to the animals, then walked over to the saloon.

He was greeted with the pleasantly familiar scents of beer and sawdust when he entered the place. The saloon was empty except for the bartender, who smiled a welcome.

"You would be the marshal we heard was in town," the barkeep said. "Marshal Long, is it?" Small towns, bless them. There were no secrets here.

"That's right. Custis Long, but my friends call me Longarm. Some o' my enemies do also, so you might as well, too." He extended his hand to the bartender in the apron.

That gentleman said, "I'm Tyrone Boetcher. I'm pleased to meet you, Longarm. What can I do for you?"

"First thing would be information," Longarm said.

Boetcher shook his head. "Sam already told me about those five men. I wish I could help, but there has been no such group in here. Two days ago, though . . . I think it was two, might have been three . . . I had a couple customers who could have been two of them."

"Did you see any more? Outside maybe?"

"Not that I noticed, and there was no little girl with them. I'm positive about that. I would have heard if any such group passed through. Of course the others could have camped out away from town to keep the girl out of sight."

"Did these two buy whiskey to carry along with them?"

Boetcher nodded. "They did. Half a case. They had me stuff in more shavings to fill the box."

"Like they were going to pack it on a mule," Longarm said.

"Yep. That's why I mention it. Could be these were your kidnappers. Something else that fits. Sam and I talked about them. The same time as the two were in here buying whiskey, he had one stranger in his place buying food. Seems like a mighty odd coincidence. If it was a coincidence," Boetcher said.

Longarm grunted. "I've learned to mistrust coincidences, friend. I'm betting you and Sam were right. They almost had to be part of the gang. An' the other two laid out somewhere so Tina wouldn't be spotted."

"You say that like you know the girl," Boetcher observed.

"I do. She calls me Uncle Custis. She . . . trusts me. I promised her mama I'd bring her home. I figure t' do that, Mr. Boetcher. Alive or dead, I figure t' take her home. An' I'll see in Hell the men who've hurt her. I promised her mama that, too."

Longarm sighed. "D'you know how damn frustrating it is t' have to set here an' wait? I want t' jump in the saddle and set out at a run. But where? In what damn direction? Shit!"

"Would you like something to drink while you wait?" Boetcher suggested.

"Sure." Longarm looked skeptically at the back bar where a few dusty bottles were displayed. "D'you have . . . ?"

"Whatever it is, Longarm, we don't have it. Those are all full of water with some food color added. We have some keg whiskey . . . not bad for what it is but still keg whiskey . . . and we have a pretty decent beer. Take your pick from those."

"In that case why don't I have a glass o' that good keg whiskey and a beer chaser. An' do you have a deck o' cards so's I can lay out a little solitaire on one o' your tables?"

"Go ahead and sit down. I'll bring your drinks and a fresh deck of cards right away." When Longarm reached into his pocket, Boetcher added, "No charge, Longarm. We all want you to find that little girl. You don't owe a thing in my place of business."

"Funny thing," Longarm said. "Just when I get to feeling overwhelmed with how shitty human beings can be, I get a reminder that folks can be almighty kind as well. Folks like you an' Sam an' Mrs. Collins."

Boetcher laughed. "Amanda. Now she's something special, isn't she?"

"I have to agree, sir. Indeed I do." Longarm chose a table near the back of the place and sat down. Tyrone Boetcher had the drinks and the cards in front of him right away.

Longarm reached first for the whiskey. Then for the beer. Finally for the packet of playing cards. He broke the seal with his thumbnail, lit a cheroot, and began to shuffle the deck.

Chapter 27

"Marshal Long?"

Longarm looked up to see a skinny kid of fourteen or so with freckles and a shock of wheat-straw hair that stuck out in all directions. "That's me. What can I do for you?"

"Sam Johnson, sir. He told me to tell you there's a message coming in for you."

"On my way." Longarm threw a quick thank-you at Tyrone Boetcher and was out the door before the boy was.

By the time Longarm reached Johnson's store, the message was complete.

MAY HAVE ONE YOU WANT COME SOONEST

It was signed by Justice of the Peace Charles Mayweather, Upton, Kansas.

Longarm read it, then looked at Johnson. "I never heard of any Upton, Kansas. Where is it?"

"North and a little west from here. It's about, oh, sixty miles or so."

"Is there a road or would it all be across country?"

"There's a road. This one that we're on. It goes through

Upton, then on all the way to the Union Pacific tracks. We haul all our goods in over this road so it's pretty well maintained."

"Good." Longarm checked his Ingersoll watch. It was past five o'clock. Before long, it would be dark. "Do me a favor, Sam. Put me up a bundle of food. Jerky, hard biscuits, whatever can be grabbed an' eaten while in the saddle. I'm gonna go over to Mrs. Collins' place an' get my clothes. I'll pick up the food on my way back an' be out o' here in two shakes."

"It will be ready for you," Johnson promised.

Longarm was as good as his word, although Amanda Collins did convince him to roll his clothes into a bundle that he could tie behind his saddle. The rough hand-me-down things he was wearing would be better for travel. That would also get him on his way a few minutes quicker.

"Thanks." He hesitated only for a moment—the woman was plump and plain and much older than he—then gave her a good-bye kiss and headed fast back to the mercantile.

Johnson had a set of old saddlebags already stuffed with jerky and cured sausages along with slabs of hardtack and some salt pork. "I know the pork will need cooking, but take it anyway," the storekeeper said. "There's some ready-ground coffee in there, too. You won't be traveling all the time. If nothing else, the horses will need to rest every now and then."

"They can rest after we get to Upton," Longarm said on his way out the door.

He saddled quickly and arranged his gear so the balance would not upset the gait of whichever horse he was riding at a given moment, then swung into the McClellan. The horse thought about getting snorty with him, but Longarm quickly put an end to that. He was not in the mood for it. As soon as the animal settled, Longarm touched his spurs to it and cantered out onto the road.

The sun was almost down to the horizon by then. Longarm adjusted the set of his Stetson and dropped his chin to keep it out of his eyes.

This figured to be a long, hard night, but at least he had the wagon road to follow now, and that he could easily do in the dark.

Upton, Kansas, was not much bigger than the flyspeck he just left. Longarm reached it just before dawn, switching back and forth between the horses and pushing them as hard as he pushed himself. He wanted the cocksuckers who took Tina. Wanted them bad.

When Longarm arrived, there was lamplight showing in just one window on the main street. A sign beside the door said BURL'S CAFÉ, GOOD EATS.

Longarm wearily climbed down from the saddle, his legs stiff and joints complaining. He tied the horses to a railing and stepped up onto the board walkway in front of the café. He paused there to light a cheroot, his next to last, and cussed himself for forgetting to replenish his supply of smokes when he had the chance back in Sam Johnson's store.

A tiny bell over the door rang when he pushed the door open. A bearded, heavy-set man wearing a sparkling clean apron looked around from the stove where he was busy tending a dozen or so thin pork steaks.

"You're up and about early, mister," the man said in greeting.

"Reckon I could say the same about you."

"Oh, I'm here at this hour every morning."

"Then you must be Burl."

"That's right. Burl Burmeister. And you would be . . . ?"

Longarm gave his name and said, "I'm looking for a Charles Mayweather."

Burmeister nodded. "Charlie is our blacksmith. He is, um, busy right now. Mind if I ask what your business is with him?"

"I mind," Longarm said.

"No offense, it's just that we, um, have this situation in town at the moment."

"Situation?"

"Charlie is over at the smithy. He has a fella detained there. Chained inside a stall in the barn actually. We don't have a proper jail, you see."

"Lots of towns don't. But what is this 'situation' as you call it?"

"It's just . . . a bunch of the fellows want to hang this fellow."

"What's he guilty of?"

"Well, now, you see, that's the thing. We all know what he done. It's just that he hasn't been tried in a proper court of law. And Charlie, he doesn't have that sort of authority. He isn't even a sworn-in justice of the peace. That's just what we asked him to do. He handles complaints and levies fines for nitpicky shit like somebody being drunk in public or what-have-you, but he isn't a for-real JP. He says it wouldn't be right for this fella to hang except he's found guilty by a real judge. That's why he's over there trying to make sure nobody hauls this bastard out and lynches him first."

"You say everybody knows what this man done. What was it?"

"Well, he . . . he up and molested a girl. Young girl. And that's another thing. Some of the fellows got to worrying that if the fellow is taken to a regular court, that little girl will have to sit in front of a jury and testify to the things that were done to her. That would be terrible. We all agree about that. It would be like her being molested all over again. Do you see what I mean?"

"I do," Longarm said. "This girl. Is she from around here?" For a moment there, he had hope.

But Burl said, "Yes, her and her family live here in Upton. Why?"

"Just a thought. Where can I find Justice Mayweather and the accused?"

"The smithy is over in that direction, right on the edge of town. You can't miss it. Or you could wait until the sun comes up and folks start to stir again. The men, most of them, got pretty drunk last night, but I figure as soon as they wake up, they'll be yammering for that poor bastard's hide again. You mark my words, Mr. Long. By mid-morning, he's apt to be food for the magpies."

"Do me a favor if you would, please. I see some soft rolls that look awful nice. Stick a chunk o' that pork inside one and give it to me, would you? I don't have time t' eat it here. Not if I intend t' stop a hanging, I don't."

"Mister, it would take more than one man to stop a lynch mob."

Longarm grimaced. "Depends on the man. Now hand me that pork sandwich, please. I'm in a bit of a hurry."

Chapter 28

Justice of the Peace Charles Mayweather was a stocky man with a bushy beard and bald dome. He stood guard at the entrance to the smithy, holding a heavy steel hammer for a weapon. Years of swinging that hammer had left him with muscles in places where Longarm was not sure he even had places. Even so, a hammer was not much of a mob deterrent.

But then Mayweather surely knew that. The hammer was for show, and likely he had no intention of using it if push came to shove. If he were serious, he would have a large-bore shotgun in hand.

Longarm stepped into the spill of light from a lantern hanging over the door. He held his hand well away from the butt of his Colt and said, "Are you Mayweather?"

"I am. Now who would you be?"

"Deputy U.S. Marshal."

"You the one that wire was about?"

"I am. The men I'm looking for kidnapped a girl. I'm looking for them."

"I can't tell you if this would be one of them," Mayweather said.

"Be all right if I talk to him?"

"Go ahead."

Longarm thanked the man and went into the smithy. It smelled of iron and coal and acrid smoke. The forge looked cold and dead, but it pulsed with contained heat. The banked coke burned slowly under a thick layer of ash.

There was a stall to the right. Longarm found a lantern, struck a match, and lit it. He held it high and peered into the stall. A man wearing buckskin breeches and the scraps of what used to be a red shirt was cowering in a far corner.

The man looked like he had already met the mob that wanted to hang him. His left ear was nearly torn off, and dried blood from that wound showed black in the light from the lantern. His face and upper body were mottled with red and purple bruising. When he opened his mouth, there were gaps where teeth had recently been.

Longarm entered the stall and set the lantern aside. He introduced himself. The reaction he got from the prisoner was not a normal one.

"Thank God. You can call them bastards off and save me."

"Maybe," Longarm said. "If you're straight with me."

"Oh, yeah. Whatever you say."

"No, mister, it's what *you* say that's gonna make the difference," Longarm told him. "Now what's your name?"

"Wilson Headley. Wilse my friends call me. I was just . . . I didn't do nothing, Marshal. I was just—"

"Wilse," Longarm interrupted, "let's get one thing clear here. I already told you I expect you t' be straight. I meant that. If you ain't, if you think you can lie your way past me, I won't say a word when that mob comes. Not one word. D'you understand me? You do? Fine. I hope you mean that. An' you might want to know that the reason I'm here talkin' to you is a little girl name of Tina Washburn. Does that name mean anything to you?"

Wilson Headley took his time answering, looking off toward the ceiling as if in deep thought about the question. After a moment, he said, "No, Marshal, I don't think I ever heard that name before."

But when Longarm had mentioned Tina's name, he'd been certain he saw Headley's eyes widen—just a little— in surprise. Longarm sighed. "Oh, well. I was hopin' to get some information. Thanks for your help, Wilse. Reckon I'd best be getting back on the road now. I got t' find that little girl." He turned and headed toward the gate.

"Where are you going?"

"I told you. I'm looking for Tina Washburn. I got no time to waste here if you don't know anything to help me find her."

"But . . . you can't. That mob. Those men. What about them?"

"They aren't none o' my affair," Longarm said. "That's up to the local law. I got no jurisdiction here."

"They'll kill me," Headley wailed. He sounded like he was about to cry.

"Yes," Longarm said. "They likely will. Now excuse me, please. I got to get moving."

"No, I . . . what do you want to know?"

"Everything," Longarm said. "I want t' know everything. Starting with whether the girl is still alive. If she isn't, I'll want t' know where I can find her body. But I'm telling you true. I want t' know *every*thing."

There were six of them, until a soldier they jumped in an alley in Tascosa knifed one in the belly. Then there were five. Not friends exactly. They banded together for the strength that came from numbers. They made their way through strong-arm robbery and intimidation.

In addition to Wilse Headley, there was Lewis Crane, Roman Turner, Bobby Allison, and Nelson Gambrel. There were no choirboys among them, but Turner and Gambrel were far and away the most vicious of them. Turner had held Teddy down while Gambrel cut his belly open. He said he just wanted to see what was inside such a gutless little dirt-grubbing bastard.

Rape was their pleasure. It was also the reason they had to keep moving. If they stayed too long in any one area, they surely would have wound up hanging from a sturdy tree limb or a handy telegraph pole.

Headley swore Tina was still alive the last he saw of the group. She was the reason they did not all come into a town together. Someone had to stay in camp to watch her lest she try to escape or, worse, tell someone what was happening to her. They would kill her rather than risk letting people learn they took her against her will.

The reason they had not killed her or simply beaten and left her long before now, as they normally did with their victims, was that Turner fancied himself in love with the girl.

Roman Turner Nellie, Headley said, had some idea that he could get Tina to fall in love with him, too, and they would live happily ever after.

"Like in some sort of fucking fairy tale. You know?"

Headley had come into Upton together with Lewis Crane. The two of them bought the things they needed, then started back to camp. They would have been all right, except school was just letting out at the time and Wilson Headley saw a girl he wanted. Crane headed back to camp alone while Headley stayed behind to stalk the girl.

Yes, he baldly admitted, it was his intention to fuck her. But she was no kid. She must have been fifteen or sixteen.

Back home, he said, she would have been married and had a kid or two of her own by then.

His bad luck was her boyfriend, who came up behind while Headley was rooting around on top of the girl. The boyfriend picked up a rock and smashed Headley with it.

When he told about that, Headley reached back and fingered a blood-crusted split in his scalp. "Son of a bitch like to brained me. Until you came along, I woulda considered that a blessing." He sneered. "But I told you everything. I told you true, just like you said, and now you got to protect me from these crazy bastards."

"You haven't told me quite everything yet. I want to know where they were headed from here," Longarm said.

"North. We didn't have no special destination in mind. Hell, we didn't none of us know this country or what towns are in it. We just sorta ride along and look for whatever we find. Men we rob. Women we fuck. And rob, too, of course."

"Of course."

"Hey! Where the hell are you going?"

Longarm paused. "North," he said without bothering to turn to face Headley again.

"But . . . what about me?"

"What about you?"

"I can hear them coming. Can't you hear that?"

"Yeah," Longarm said. "I can hear."

And he could. Somewhere close by, he could hear the angry, growing growl of an approaching mob. It was a low, animal sound. Ugly and terrifying.

"You got to get me out of here. You got to take me. I'm your prisoner. I confess. Whatever you want me to say, I confess. But don't let those bastards get me. That asshole with the hammer can't stop them. He doesn't really want to stop them. He told me so. He's just . . . you got to take me with you, Marshal. You got to!"

Longarm pulled out a cheroot—it was his last; he would have to stop at a store and buy some more cigars on his way out of town—and extracted a match from his pocket. He used his teeth to nip the twist from the cheroot, snapped the match aflame with his thumbnail, and lit that final cheroot.

"Where are you going? Stop!" he heard behind him.

"I already told you," he called back over his shoulder. "This ain't my jurisdiction." He lengthened his stride as he reached the street. He did not look back.

Chapter 29

Four men, five packhorses, and a girl. Heading somewhere toward the north. It was not much information, but it was more than he had known before.

The packhorses, Headley said, carried plunder from their robberies. Whatever their victims had, the group would take. If they could not use an item, perhaps they could sell or swap it later. They would steal almost anything of value.

And Tina. She was still alive.

The remaining four did not know they were being chased, but they would be wary nonetheless. They were fugitives everywhere they had been.

But Tina was alive.

Longarm went back to Burl's Café to pay for the sandwich he'd already taken, and to grab another one along with a cup of coffee, then tried to find a store where he could buy a few cigars. He could find a store all right, two of them in fact, but they were still closed. Either it was too early for the storekeepers to open, or the proprietors were with the lynch mob over at the smithy.

The smithy was several blocks away, but he could hear

the shouting. Anger at first. Then the sounds lessened. It became quiet over there.

Until a roar of triumph went up.

Longarm did not have to see to know that Wilson Headley was at that moment plunging down into the fiery depths of Hell. Hands tied, legs thrashing, tongue protruding, eyes bulging, piss and shit flowing out of his body.

Longarm had seen many more than his fair share of hangings. A proper execution performed by a hangman who knew his trade was ugly enough, but at least then the hanged man fell a distance carefully calculated to snap his neck and cause instant death.

He had seen a few lynchings, too, and those went beyond ugly. There was no drop. Just an upward pull lifting the person off the ground. The hanged man strangled slowly, painfully. It could take the lynched man a long time to die, a very long time if he had strong muscles in his neck.

Headley had looked like a man who might suffer for quite a while before he finally went under.

Not as long as Teddy-something suffered, though.

Longarm abandoned his search for cigars. He did not have time for that luxury. He switched his McClellan to the other horse and buckled the cinch tight, then swung into the saddle.

He could still hear the mob behind him as he guided his horses out of town. Heading north.

Chapter 30

Longarm drew rein beside the shining steel of the railroad tracks. The horses dropped their heads, seemingly as bone weary as he was. Both animals were near to being played out. He needed to replace them.

Hell, he needed lots of things. Most of all, he needed to get a line on where the kidnappers were now. Over the past few days, he had lost them. He knew they were going north, but there was a helluva lot of north up there where they could be.

It might have been possible to track them if there had been any rain lately. As it was, the hard, dry ground yielded no information.

But he did know one thing that he hadn't been sure of. Reaching the Union Pacific tracks meant that sometime in the past few days he'd left Kansas and crossed into Nebraska.

He stepped down from the saddle and stretched, arching his back and swinging his arms. He stared rather enviously at the line of telegraph poles that ran for literally hundreds of miles beside the UP tracks.

Those thin wires could put him in communication with a

wide network of lawmen. The problem was that the lineman's telegraph key he always carried in his bag was still in the upstairs bedroom back at Mae Washburn's boardinghouse back in Colorado City, along with the rest of his gear.

Longarm sighed. He had choices to make. And if he chose the wrong course, it was Tina Washburn who would suffer.

No, that was not right. The girl was already suffering. There was nothing Custis Long could do now to wipe that away. The best he could hope for was to put an end to it.

If she still lived.

He gathered the reins and stepped into his saddle. The brown horse tossed its head and tried to resume cropping the scant, dry sprigs of tough grass.

Longarm tossed a mental coin and reined west. He needed fresh horses and updated information.

He needed a town and a telegraph key.

Longarm ignored his own needs and rode straight to the tiny shack that served the railroad's needs here. There would be a telegraph operator in there to receive train orders so the proper signals could be displayed.

There was a scruffy old fellow with tobacco stains in his mustache seated beside a checkerboard studying on his next move. His opponent, if he had one, was not in evidence. Longarm's arrival broke the oldster's concentration. He looked up from the board and said, "I don't sell tickets here, mister. Go over to Todd Lancaster's store. He'll fix you up."

"I'm not looking t' buy a ticket," Longarm told him. "I need t' send some wires. Two actually. One t' be copied to every receiving station in a hundred miles east, west, or north from here. The other to U.S. Marshal William Vail in

Denver. Now where's a message pad and a pencil so's I can write it down for you?"

Twenty minutes later, Longarm led his tired horses onto the main street of whatever tiny town this was. He tied them outside Lancaster's store and went in.

"How can I help you, mister?"

"Friend, I got more needs than a kid has wishes on Christmas morning. But let's start with some cigars, cheroots if you have 'em. I haven't had anything t' smoke for days now."

"I have a good-quality cheroot."

"Fine. Let me have a dollar's worth. Matches to go with 'em. Balbriggans. You got any balbriggans about my size?"

Lancaster nodded.

"Good. I ain't hardly had these off in the past couple weeks an' they're commencing to rot clean off me, I think. Um, socks, too, if you have any. The ones I'm wearing are in even worse shape than the balbriggans. An' is there any place in town where I can get a haircut and a bath? I need both something awful."

"I, uh, would have to agree," Lancaster said, wrinkling his nose and scowling. Not that Longarm could blame the man. At this point, the horses smelled better than he did. And that one hard-mouthed son of a bitch smelled pretty ripe.

Lancaster gave him directions to the town barber, and began to pull brown paper off the roll behind his counter.

"No, no need t' wrap those things. I'll take them just like they are," Longarm told the storekeeper.

He plucked a cheroot from the little bundle that Lancaster handed him, struck a match, and drew the smoke long and deep into his lungs.

And damned near coughed his lungs out.

After going without a cigar for days, now the smoke was harsh in his throat and bitter on his tongue.

He drew in on the cheroot again, more slowly this time, and that was better. Another minute or so, and the smoke tasted as good as he remembered it should.

He took a few more minutes to ask Lancaster if he had seen any of the kidnappers. If so, they'd made no impression and he could not remember them, nor had he seen Tina.

Longarm paid for his purchases and went back out to the horses. He put the cheroots away in his saddlebags, then took his own clothes down from behind the saddle. They were still rolled and tied, just the way Mrs. Collins had done them up for him. The borrowed things could be discarded. They were quite as ripe as he was.

"Gimme the works," Longarm told the white-haired barber. "Bath, haircut, shave, everything."

"In there," the barber told him, pointing. "You're in luck. Fresh water today. But . . . I don't know. I probably should charge you extra. No offense, mister, but once you've been washed in that water, I don't think I could use it again for anyone else."

"That's all right. I'll pay for your clean water."

"In that case, go on in there and strip. I'll bring a bucket of hot water straight away."

Nothing—well, nothing that did not involve a naked woman—could possibly feel as good as that hot bath did.

Chapter 31

Damn but it felt good to be clean again and in clean clothes that actually fit. He must have washed off five pounds of dirt and sweat in there. It was worthwhile paying for the fresh water.

He stopped for a moment to light another cheroot, then walked over to the railroad shack to see if there were any responses that would put him back on the trail of the kidnappers. Thank goodness for modern conveniences, Longarm reflected as he walked. Without the telegraph, these miserable assholes might be able to slip away unscathed.

He intended to see that no such thing happened this time.

"Any returns?" he asked, poking his head into the shack.

The signalman swung his swivel chair around to see who was speaking, then leaned forward and picked up a sheaf of message forms. The man shuffled through them, then selected one that he held out to Longarm. "Just this one," he said.

Longarm thanked the man and glanced down at the yellow sheet in his hand. It was from Billy Vail back in Denver. Short and succinct.

It was, of course, true. Kidnapping was not a federal crime, and he knew it.

On the other hand, dammit, he was *not* going to abandon Tina to those bastards.

If she was alive, he would find and free her. If she was already dead—and that was a distinct possibility given the sort of men these were—he would see to it that they never again were able to hurt some other innocent girl.

If he had to give up his badge, he intended to follow the sons of bitches and bring every one of them to justice. The law's justice. Or his own, if that was the way it played out.

But he was *not* going to turn his back on that little girl.

The message on the telegram in his hand was something he had been thinking about for days.

"I'd like to send a return, please," he told the telegrapher.

The man picked up a pencil and said, "All right, shoot."

Slowly, to make sure he did not get ahead of the signalman, he said, "Suspects may be involved postal robberies Texas and New Mexico. Stop. In close pursuit. Stop."

Close pursuit was stretching things a mite. But what the hell.

"Anything else?" the telegrapher asked.

Longarm thought about it for a moment, then shook his head. "I reckon that covers it."

"All right. I'll get this on the wire right now." He swung his chair back around and opened his key.

Chapter 32

Longarm could use a glass of rye whiskey to go with his cheroots, but he wanted to be ready if—no, dammit, not if, *when*—a response came from one of those telegrams.

Tina's kidnappers were not invisible. They were the sort who would be trouble wherever they traveled. Someone had to have seen them. Longarm's only problem was in finding that someone and getting a lead on the kidnappers again.

The word would come, though. He believed that. If only because it *had* to come for Tina's sake.

When it did come, he intended to be ready.

Before the rye, before his first decent meal in days, he had to be sure he was ready to hit the saddle and move again.

He gathered the reins of his two ex-cavalry horses and led the gaunt and footsore animals down the street to a livery and feed store on the edge of town.

"Yo. Anybody home here?"

"Down in a minute," a voice answered from above. Moments later, there was a cascade of dust, dirt, and dry, broken hay stems falling through the opening where a ladder led up to the hayloft. A pair of shoes and blue jeans appeared, followed by the figure of a tall, bearded man.

The fellow was probably in his forties. His hair had begun to go gray. He rubbed his hands together to brush off any dirt, then extended his right hand to Longarm. "Henry Wiggin," he said.

Wiggin eyed Longarm's horses, then said, "Those animals are about used up, mister. They need two, maybe three weeks of rest and good feed to get some meat back on them and put some strength in them again."

Longarm nodded. "That's exactly right and it's what I'd sure do if I had the time to spare, but I don't. So I've come t' make a swap. I need fresh horses."

The easy thing would be for him to sign a government voucher and have the Department of Justice pay for whatever he needed. Except he was already skating on thin ice with Billy Vail about this very personal manhunt he was on.

Billy might refuse to honor a voucher. He had every right to do so, this effort having been authorized by no one but Longarm himself.

But Longarm needed fresh horses. Needed them bad.

"Let me tell you *why* I need to make a trade," Longarm said.

Five minutes later, Henry Wiggin sighed and said, "I suppose you have proof about this story you've told me."

"No, sir, I do not. I can show you my credentials as a deputy U.S. marshal, but I'm not carryin' any warrants or posters about the four men nor anything on paper about the child."

"All right, let me see those," Wiggin said.

Longarm dragged out his wallet and opened it for the man.

Wiggin grunted. "I suppose you know you could just sign a voucher for anything you need here."

"Yes, sir, but my boss doesn't yet know what I'm up to. He hasn't authorized the use of vouchers, and if I sign one there would be a chance . . . a small one but a chance . . . that you wouldn't get paid. I wouldn't do that to you. And I don't have much cash money with me. Certainly not enough to buy horses from you. That's why I'm asking for a swap."

"You have papers on these horses?"

"No, sir, I do not." Longarm explained to the man the circumstances of his getting the horses.

"Dammit, Marshal, you do put a man in a hard place here," Wiggin complained.

"I apologize, Mr. Wiggin. I'll just . . . maybe I can find someone in town who wants to buy them. You know. T' give me cash so's I can deal on something else."

"I said you put a man in a hard place, and you do. If I make a trade with you, it will be at least two weeks before I can think about getting my money back. If I don't make a trade, I'll have to spend that long and a whole lot more thinking about that little girl and calling myself a son of a bitch for not helping when I could."

"Does that mean you'll trade with me?" Longarm asked.

Wiggin scowled. "Yeah, it does. Look around. Pick out whatever you like. I'll trade you even up."

Longarm smiled. "Thank you, sir."

Chapter 33

Longarm led his horses—a short, compact grulla and a blood bay—down the street and tied them in front of a saloon that had a dozen or so other mounts already waiting there. The amount of business being done inside was a reminder that the day was getting short. It was time for workingmen to knock off and think about supper and a drink.

He paused on the sidewalk, then spun around and crossed the street, heading for the railroad and the signal shack.

"No, Marshal. Sorry."

"Shit." Longarm crossed back over to the saloon, and this time went in. He chose a spot at the far end of the bar and leaned on an elbow so he could observe the men in the place.

This was obviously a drinking man's establishment. There were no gaming tables, no whores, and no piano player. Just beer and whiskey. The barkeep looked like he bathed regularly. The first day of every summer. Longarm doubted that he washed his apron that often. Still, it was not the view that he came here for.

"What's yours, mister?"

"D'you have any rye?"

"Fuck, no."

"Bonded whiskey?"

"Not hardly."

"In that case, I'll have a beer," Longarm told him. Not that he mistrusted the quality of the alcohol being served here, but . . . he didn't want to chance it anyway.

The beer had too much head on it, but better too much foam than none. At least it wasn't flat. Longarm dipped his mustache in the suds, and found that it tasted pretty good, fresh beer being one of the advantages of having access to the railroad.

It would have been foolish to expect to see any of Tina's kidnappers here. Entirely too much coincidence to be possible. But he could not help looking at the others who were lined up along the bar or sitting at one of the two tables in the place.

No one even came close to matching the very sketchy descriptions he had gotten of Crane, Turner, Allison, and Gambrel.

There was one fellow Longarm's gaze kept returning to, though. He was sitting at the table playing some card game or other with two other men, all of them well dressed in suits and string ties.

The one—"Son of a bitch!" Longarm muttered.

Sidney Pike. Wanted in Kansas for mail fraud and a long string of state charges as well.

If this was indeed Sidney Pike.

If he was Pike, he should have a scar under his ear on the right side of his neck. Where he sat now, Longarm could see the left side of his face. Pike was sitting more or less in the corner so that it would be obvious as hell if Longarm were to sidle in beside him.

But then why not? If he was Pike, Longarm could put the arm on him. If he was just some innocent townsman,

Longarm could simply smile and pretend to be watching the play.

Longarm took a pull at his beer and set the mug down. He headed for the table where Pike and the other two were seated.

Pike looked up. His eyes narrowed.

Longarm never did know how he gave himself away, but Pike caught on that he was a target before Longarm had taken three steps.

Pike grabbed the underside of the flimsy card table and heaved. Cards and drinks flew, and one of the other men at the table fell over backward, his chair breaking into splinters when it hit the floor. The other man shouted and leaped out of the way.

The confidence man from Kansas ducked behind the overturned table, dropping out of Longarm's line of sight for a moment. When he popped back into view, he had a revolver in his hand.

The bastard wasted no time with warnings. He triggered a shot across the room, and immediately ducked out of sight again. Someone behind Longarm screamed.

Men scattered and glassware flew.

Longarm held his fire. He had no target, and the man whose chair had overturned was trying to scramble up.

Pike's gun hand appeared over the top rim of the table and triggered another wild, unaimed shot in Longarm's general direction. Behind Longarm, someone cussed, but he could not tell if it was because the man had been hit by Pike's wild bullet or if he was simply pissed off at the disruption.

Pike fired again, the slug striking somewhere behind the bar. Glassware shattered—bottles, glasses, the mirror, something—and shards of broken glass flew.

"Fuck this," Longarm mumbled. He did not want any more bystanders hit by bullets, or by flying glass either for that matter.

And that tabletop damn sure was not thick enough to stop a .44 slug.

He judged where Sidney Pike's chest would likely be, aimed, and fired.

Longarm heard a grunt of pain, so he aimed and fired twice more in roughly the same spot.

This time, the shooting was followed by a muted thump as something heavy fell to the floor.

Longarm's ears were ringing from the repeated explosions inside the saloon, and his vision was clouded by the billows of white smoke that still hung in the air. The sulfur and charcoal stink of burnt powder filled his nose. He knew from experience that he would be smelling it for days to come.

It never ceased to amaze him that gun smoke, which smelled so good when in the open air, could stink so when it was contained in a small space.

"What the fuck was that all about?" the barkeep—and presumably the saloon's owner—asked. He had to repeat the question twice to get through the buzzing in Longarm's head. Even then, it sounded like the man was speaking through cotton wool.

"U.S. marshal," Longarm said. "He's wanted. Must've recognized me somehow."

"Why are you just standing there? Are you just going to let him die there?"

"Mister, if he's dead it won't hurt him none t' lie there a little longer. If he ain't dead, well, I don't want t' take any chances that he might have life enough left in him to get one more shot off." Longarm turned his attention to a tall, lean man who was sitting on the floor with his back to the bar. The fellow was holding his shattered left arm, obviously a result of Pike's first bullet, the one that had been too hastily aimed at Longarm.

Longarm knelt beside the tall man. "Are you all right, mister?"

"I will be. Help me up, will you, please."

Longarm helped the man to his feet. Two others, friends apparently, came forward—finally—to help get him to a doctor.

Once they were safely outside, Longarm said, "All the rest of you had best leave for a little while, too. We don't know if that fella over there is dead or just playin' possum."

The room quickly cleared at that thought. Even the barkeep scooted out from behind his own bar and out the door.

Finally, when he was alone in the saloon, Longarm moved to his right close to the wall. From there he could get a look, a partial look anyway, behind the overturned table.

Pike lay on his right side, curled into a fetal position. Longarm could see his left hand. But not his right hand nor his revolver.

Longarm took one careful step forward. Then another. If he could only get a better look.

He almost got too good a look. While he was peering at Pike's feet, hoping to see if he could spot any movement, Pike damned near nailed him.

The confidence man sat bolt upright, his chest a mass of red from the blood still pouring out of his wounds. He raised his pistol. It seemed to take all the waning strength he could muster.

Probably he would not have enough strength left to aim and fire again.

139

Probably.

Longarm had not stayed alive this time by relying on "probably." He lifted his Colt and put a .44 slug into Sidney Pike's left temple, shattering the man's skull and sending gray brains squirting out past his eyeballs.

It was ugly. But then most violent death is.

Longarm took his time about reloading the Colt. Pike was no threat to anyone now.

. Chapter 34

Longarm saw the twin tubes of a large-bore shotgun peek through the batwings. He held his Colt ready, but the man who came into view behind the shotgun muzzles wore a badge on his chest. Even so, Longarm kept the Colt at the ready. It would be terrible to be shot down by a felon. It would be even worse to be shot accidentally by some local lawman.

"U.S. marshal," Longarm said, holding his badge up in his left hand.

The town marshal relaxed. The shotgun tubes tilted down toward the floor.

The man walked over to the corner and looked behind the overturned card table. What he saw there made him turn pale and he gagged a little, trying to keep from puking. When he turned toward Longarm again, Longarm had his revolver back in the leather and was lighting a cheroot in a doomed attempt to get the smell of gunpowder out of his nostrils.

"Jesse Walker," the marshal announced himself. "I'm, uh, I make saddles, straps, belts, anything in leather." Which would explain the dyes on his fingers. Perhaps that was the reason he did not offer to shake hands.

"Uh-huh." Longarm's introduction was brief. If Walker did not want to be friendly, that was his affair.

"I heard there was a federal man in town," Walker said. "What business do you have here?"

"Government business."

"You're looking for four men and a young girl."

"Then you already know what my business is," Longarm said.

"Don't you know you are required to present yourself to local authorities when you attempt to conduct searches inside a duly authorized legal jurisdiction?"

Longarm had had just about enough of this bullshit. "Don't you know that if you get in my way I'll take that bird-shooter away from you an' shove it up your ass?"

Walker turned shades of red darkening to purple. "Why . . . why . . . why—" Whatever else he wanted to bluster, he could not seem to get it past the knots tied in his tongue.

"Now if you will excuse me, *Marshal,* I got work t' do." Walker's title came out sounding like a cuss word. Longarm brushed past him and went outside, thoroughly pissed by everything, including the fact that he'd never had time to finish his beer.

There was a crowd gathered on the sidewalk. They began scurrying back inside the saloon as soon as Longarm was past them.

Longarm walked over to the railroad shack and stuck his head in. The signalman looked up and shook his head.

"All right, thanks."

It was getting late in the day, and he was hungry for something other than his own rough trail rations. He looked up and down the street, spotted a café, and headed for it.

The place smelled of stale grease, sweat, and tobacco smoke. There were half a dozen tables and every one of them was occupied by at least two patrons. There was also a counter with low stools lined up in front of it. The stove was behind the counter along with racks of crockery, huge pots hanging overhead, and a selection of cleavers big enough to chop down timber.

The cook was a swarthy man in an apron—a much cleaner apron than the barkeep wore back in that saloon—and a white skullcap. When Longarm sat down, the man turned away from his cooking and asked, "What will it be?"

"Steak, I think. Fried taters. Coffee. Maybe a slice o' pie later. I'll let you know 'bout that," Longarm said.

The cook laughed. "Friend, you got one choice. That's pork. But you can have it one of two ways, fried or stew. Which do you want?"

"In that case, fried. And the spuds?"

"Mashed. With cream gravy."

"I couldn't think of anything nicer," Longarm told him.

The cook grinned and went back to his stove.

When he got his grub, Longarm had to admit that the man sure as hell knew what he was doing. He served a fine meal. For something that wasn't steak. And the apple pie for dessert was just as good.

Chapter 35

It was nearly dark when Longarm finished his meal and walked back out onto the street. A thin glow of lamplight showed at the single window in the railroad shack. Longarm headed for it.

If that asshole town marshal had been halfway friendly, Longarm would have let him claim the reward, if any, for Sidney Pike. As it was, he intended to make sure the United States Marshals Service got the credit, never mind that he could not reap any reward money.

He was in the middle of writing out a brief report for the telegrapher to transmit to Denver when the key chattered. Longarm could read Morse code, the standard among railroad personnel, but not as fast as this operator. Even so, he could tell that someone was responding to his request for information about the kidnappers. He put the pencil down and strained to decipher the clicks coming through the wire.

"Here it is, Marshal." The telegraph operator sounded as proud as if he himself was responsible for the success. He swung his chair around, a broad smile on his face, and handed Longarm the flimsy.

THREE MEN ANSWERING DESCRIP ONE
NAMED ROMAN ANOTHER GAMBLE STAYING
HOTEL HERE STOP ADVISE SOONEST SIGNED
RIVERS

Gamble, Longarm thought. That would be Gambrel.
Roman would be Turner. But only three of them. And no
mention of a girl.

Longarm's heart sank anew at the thought of the news
he would have to carry back to Mae Washburn.

One thing he damn sure intended to be able to tell the
child's mother was that Tina's . . . kidnappers—he could
not bring himself to think of them as her killers—had been
brought to justice.

"D'you know where this place is?" he asked, staring at
the flimsy in his hand.

The operator shook his head. "No, sir, I don't."

"All right then. Thanks. Thank you very much." Longarm stuck the paper in his pocket and headed out the door.

His horses were still standing tied outside the saloon
where he had left them earlier. They were rested and ready.
He yanked the cinch tight and stepped onto the grulla, then
leaned down and untied the bay's lead rope from the hitch
rail.

He wheeled left and took them at a walk down to the
livery where the hostler was friendly. The man was sitting
outside enjoying a pipe and the evening air.

"Hello again, Marshal. Is there something wrong with
those horses?"

"No, sir. This time I'm needin' directions. You know of
a place named, uh, named Alvarez?"

"Sure. It's about thirty-odd miles north of here. Small-
ish sort of place. Mixed folks there. Some cows, small

146

farms, civilized Indians. A little of this and not much of that, if you know what I mean."

"The sort of place where strangers would stand out, though," Longarm said.

"Yes, I'd say they would."

"And how would I go about getting there?"

"All their goods come in on the rails and are carried by wagon road straight up to Alvarez. If you go down past the bank and turn left, that road will take you right to it. If those horses hold up as well as I think they will, you can be there before midnight tonight. Noon tomorrow if you wait till daybreak to start off."

"Are these animals reliable in the dark?" Longarm asked.

Henry Wiggin shrugged and pointed the stem of his pipe at the bay. "I know for a fact that that'un is. I won't make promises about the grulla because I don't know."

"Fair enough. An' I thank you for all your help." Longarm touched the brim of his Stetson in salute and reined the grulla off toward the bank. Turn left there, the man said, and follow the wagon road.

As soon as he reached the edge of town, Longarm lightly touched his spurs to the grulla's flanks and squeezed with his knees. He wanted speed out of these two. Just not so much speed that he used them up.

Now if only the kidnappers were there in Alvarez.

Chapter 36

He reached the community of Alvarez well before midnight, switching horses twice on the way and walking them for five minutes at each changeover. He judged the animals would have been good for another fast thirty miles had he needed them.

In the dark, he could not get much of a look at Alvarez, but he got the impression there was little to it. The only lights he could see came from the windows and open doorway of a building at the near edge of town. Longarm stopped there and dismounted. He tied his horses with the dozen or so already snubbed to the hitching posts there, and took a moment to stretch and loosen his muscles after hours in the saddle.

The scent of beer and the whirring clatter of a slot machine announced the sort of business that was conducted here. Longarm stopped at the doorway to take a look before he went inside.

The place was doing a good trade considering the late hour. The patrons seemed to be a mix of working-class town folks and cowhands. The best way to tell them apart was to look at their feet. Town people tend to wear shoes.

Cowhands will virtually always wear boots. About half of the men in the place were armed.

A few whores in short dresses and painted smiles mingled with the crowd.

The bar was at the back of the room. Two card tables and a faro layout occupied most of the floor space, and there were three one-armed bandits at the far right end. One table and two of the slot machines were in use at the moment.

Longarm knew if he stayed in the doorway too long, he would draw unwanted attention to himself, so he went to the bar and propped a foot on the brass rail. He bought a beer and helped himself to a pickled egg and a handful of peanuts from the free lunch spread.

He watched the crowd through the mirror behind the bar so it would not be obvious that he was staring.

The information he had about the four men was very sketchy, but they were all reported to have beards. Of course, a man could always take a notion to shave, but it was not likely. More than half the men in the saloon were clean-shaven and probably not of interest.

Of those who were bearded, two were gray-haired and four were not armed. That left two, one who had had much too much to drink and one who was feeding coins into a slot machine.

The man at the slot machine could have been Lewis Crane. He was tall enough, with a turkey neck and barn-door ears. In addition to a revolver, he carried a long, curved skinning knife at his belt. With those long arms, he could be a formidable opponent in a knife fight. If he knew what he was doing.

Not that Longarm intended getting into a knife fight with

the man. Let Crane—assuming this indeed was Crane—let him use a knife if he wanted to. Longarm would shoot the silly son of a bitch.

Before anything happened, though, Longarm wanted to spot the other three. Where one was, the others should not be far.

He took a sip of the beer and chewed some peanuts, then wasted more time motioning for the barkeep while he continued to look through the crowd.

"Yes, sir?"

"You got any decent cigars?"

"Of course."

"Let me have one, please, an' a match."

The bartender nodded, and a few moments later produced a dark, evil-looking thing that looked more like a turd than a cigar. He laid it and a pair of lucifers on the bar and said, "Two cents."

Longarm paid. But he suspected he was being overcharged. The management probably got these free from the outhouse in back.

The stogie did not taste quite that bad. But it wasn't good either.

Longarm sighed. As far as he could see, there was only one man in the place who could possibly be one of Tina's kidnappers, and that was the man who was still yanking the lever of the mechanical thief.

Longarm finished the pickled egg and washed it down with a swallow of beer, then approached the fellow he suspected to be Crane.

He came up behind him, stopped about six feet away, and loudly said, "Hey, Lewis, is that you?"

"Sure as hell i—" Crane was smiling when he started to

turn, but the smile froze on his face and his eyes went wide with shock when he saw Longarm standing there, Colt already in hand.

"I got some questions for you, Lewis."

Longarm could hear a thunder of swiftly moving feet as the saloon patrons suddenly realized they were late for supper and needed to get home. In a hurry.

A few scrambled over against the walls, but most managed to push and shove their way through the front door. The whores darted behind the bar and crouched down. The bartender reached underneath his bar, obviously unsure if he should bring his shotgun out or not.

"Deputy U.S. marshal," Longarm announced. "I'm gonna take this man into custody for questionin'. Right, Lewis?"

Crane snarled. His expression reminded Longarm of the look of raw nastiness he had seen once on the face of a cornered catamount. "Like hell you'll take me," Crane spat.

"On your feet or on your back," Longarm said. "It don't make any difference t' me. Now turn around an' face that bandit. Hands behind your back so's I can put the cuffs on."

"Sure I will. Sure." Crane stood where he was. Thinking perhaps. Then his eyes narrowed and Longarm knew what he had decided.

As soon as Crane's fingers touched the grips of his pistol—Longarm was wrong about him, he had not gone for the knife first—Longarm fired.

The first slug hit square in Crane's chest. It likely turned his heart to pulp, making Crane a dead man who simply did not know it yet.

Crane had strength and nerve enough to continue drawing his pistol. Probably he would not be able to cock and fire. Probably. Longarm did not chance it. He took careful aim and put a bullet in the bridge of Lewis Crane's long, thin nose.

Crane's gun never left the leather.

The pity, the way Longarm saw it, was that now he could not question the son of a bitch about Tina.

Lewis Crane had not come here alone, though. There were still three others left. And Tina, wherever she was.

Chapter 37

"That's right. Four of 'em. I seen them when they rode in t'other day. Four men. They had a woman an' two pack-horses with 'em," a lanky cowboy said.

Considering the hour, quite a crowd had gathered. They crowded into the saloon, and more were coming as word of the shooting somehow spread.

"They took up in that shack where Fred Tompkins used t' live," the cowboy said.

"This woman," Longarm asked, "could she have been young? A girl maybe?"

The cowboy shrugged. "Could be. I never seen her face. She was wearing a bonnet. You know. With the cloth sticking out like some sorta snout. You know. Like this." He demonstrated with his hands the way a bonnet shields the face from sun. "She was wearin' a dress, which is why I say t'was a woman. Female critter anyhow."

"Did she say anything?"

"None of 'em did. I wasn't all that close to them, mind. I was just riding past and seen 'em going into that shack. This fella here"—he pointed at Lewis Crane's body sprawled

in a pool of blood in front of the row of slot machines—
"was one of 'em."

"You're sure about that?"

"Oh, yeah. I recognized him earlier. He's been here all evening. Two of his friends was here, too, but they already left."

Longarm grunted. That was good news. It likely meant the rest of the gang—and Tina—would not be far.

The woman this man saw at the Tompkins shack almost had to be Tina.

It was possible that Tina was gone and they had kidnapped someone else. That, however, was not probable.

Surely, he would have heard some report of it if there had been a second kidnapping. Violence against women was almost unheard of out here in the West. Women were scarce. Perhaps because of that, they were treasured. Longarm had seen cowhands coming off months of droving who were satisfied to simply stand and stare at ladies walking past.

Day or night, a decent woman almost never had anything to fear from most Western men.

Most. Unfortunately, there was a huge difference between "most" and "all." Headley, Crane, and company were proof positive of that.

"You say this man and them others kidnapped a little girl? Is that what they done, Marshal?" another man asked.

"That's exactly what they done. They took her and murdered the boy she was with at the time." Longarm saw no need to go into long explanations about the child having been kidnapped by Teddy before this crowd kidnapped her the second time. And what he did say was true.

"Those sons o' bitches," someone barked.

A low rumble began to fill the room as word of a child's kidnapping spread. Soon there were shouts of "Kill the bastards" and "String 'em up." Longarm was afraid he had created a mob here.

"Show me where this shack is," he shouted over the growing din.

"Get a rope," someone else hollered.

"This way. Everybody this way. You, too, Marshal. We'll take you right to those cocksuckers."

The crowd, which now really had become a mob, surged out of the saloon and down the street.

Doors and windows flew open as the mob noisily marched out of town. Men, some of them still in nightshirts, poured out to join the angry locals.

Guns appeared and lanterns. A low-pitched growl rose from the mass of humanity, growing as they proceeded.

It was like the mob had become an entity of its own with a common will and a single goal. It was clear they would be satisfied with nothing less than blood. Longarm just prayed that these really were the kidnappers inside the Tompkins shack. And that Tina was with them.

Chapter 38

"Now lookahere, boys," Longarm shouted to the crowd of fifty or more rabid men, "if the girl is in there, we want t' get her out safe. Nobody shoot. Nobody do nothing. Let me talk to those men. Let me bring 'em out peaceable."

There was some muttering, but no serious objection. Longarm approached the derelict shack, Colt still in the leather and his empty hands held wide of his body so the men inside could see should they happen to be watching.

They pretty much had to be watching. Probably pissing themselves, too. There is little more terrifying than a mob. It was a fear that did not have to be learned or even understood. It was something that a man could *feel* deep in his bones.

The mere presence of a mob made the hair on the back of one's neck rise. Longarm could scarcely imagine what it must be like to be the object of a mob's collective hate.

As it was, even though the hate was directed elsewhere, he felt the weight of it when he walked forward.

The scene was lighted by torches, lanterns, even some lamps that people had carried with them from their homes. The flickering light gave an impression of unreality to it all, as if they were watching the presentation of an under-water play.

Longarm knew there was no need for him to knock to announce his arrival. He stopped outside the door and said, loudly enough for the nearer members of the mob to hear, "We'd best talk. I want you t' stay inside. I'll come in if you open the door."

"You ain't gonna shoot us down?"

"No, I won't. I'm a deputy United States marshal. It ain't my way t' shoot anybody that ain't first tryin' to shoot me. Now open up. It will be best if I can set an' talk with you."

"Just a second."

The wait was considerably longer than one second, but not nearly as long as it felt like. After what seemed like several minutes, Longarm could hear a crossbar being withdrawn and the door swung open. The occupants of the shack remained out of sight behind it.

"You say you're a deputy?"

"That's right."

"Fed'ral, not local?"

"Deputy United States marshal," Longarm repeated.

"Show me."

Longarm pulled out his wallet and flipped it open to display his badge. He still could not see anyone inside, but obviously someone was watching.

"All right. Come in. But mind now, we're armed. Don't try to play us false."

"Mister, the last thing in the world you want t' do right now is to start shootin' off guns. This crowd hears gunfire, an' it won't matter what you're shooting at. They'll tear this shack apart an' rip you t' pieces next. So was I you, I'd keep my guns cold an' my orneriness to myself. D'you understand that?"

"Yeah, you . . . Jesus!"

"I'm coming in now. Leave the door open. That might show the crowd that you got no bad intent."

Longarm turned to look at the mob behind him and signaled with a thumbs-up, then stepped inside.

The shack was little more than some scrap wood nailed upright and a flimsy excuse for a roof put overhead. There was a daub-and-wattle chimney over a small fire pit and not much else. There was no stove, no table or chairs, not even any bunks. Two blankets were laid out on the floor for sleeping.

A stub of candle burned beside the fire pit. More light strayed in through cracks in the walls, originating with the mob beyond, than was given by the guttering candle.

There were only two men in the place.

Longarm's heart sank.

There was no sign of Tina Washburn.

"First thing," he said, "who are you two? Give me your names, please."

"I'm Nelly Gambrel," the larger of the two said. "He's Bobby Allison."

Gambrel looked like he ate horseshoe nails for breakfast and farted cannon balls. He was big. He was nasty. He looked scared half to death. His companion, Bobby Allison, was sweating profusely. It was not hot inside the cabin. Allison was just that frightened. Both men obviously knew they had Death howling outside their door.

"We . . . what can we do?" Gambrel whined.

"First thing, you can tell me what you done with Tina Washburn. Is she alive? Where'd you bury her?"

161

"Mister . . . that is, um, Marshal, sir . . . we won't try and lie to you. We did find a girl. She was with some clod-kicking dirt farmer. We, well, took her with us to have a little fun. You know how it is."

"I know how it is," Longarm growled. "The thing I don't know is how it's gonna be for you two. So don't give me no bullshit. Tell me where Tina is now."

"She . . . one of the other fellas, Roman, he got the idea he was in love with the girl. He wanted her to himself. Said he knew a place where the law couldn't touch him and he was gonna take her there. Said if we tried to stop him he'd kill us. Stop him? Shit! Ain't any female worth fighting over and maybe getting killed for. We both of us told him to take her and go on."

"She is alive then," Longarm said.

"Sure. Was this morning anyway."

"Where did Turner take the girl?"

Gambrel shrugged. "He wouldn't tell us. Said it was a secret place that he knew."

Longarm looked past Gambrel's shoulder to Allison, who had been silent ever since Longarm came in. "What about you, Bobby? D'you know anything about where Roman took Tina?"

"I think . . . Roman used to be a Mormon," Allison said. "I think he might've took her with him to the mountains on west from here. I think he might've took her to the Mormon country where even your federal government can't touch him."

"You think but you're not sure, is that it?"

"Yes, sir."

"All right, I tell you what. I want you two t' turn around an' put your hands behind your backs. I'll hand . . . shit, I

162

only got one pair of handcuffs with me. You boys got any stout cord I can borrow?"

"You mean you want us to turn around and provide the means for you to capture us and take us in?"

Longarm nodded. "I do. If you got your hands secured behind you, there's a chance that crowd will let me walk you out of here. If you go out standing proud, they'll likely rip your fucking arms off you an' beat you over your stupid heads with them." Longarm took a step back. "But you do whatever you think best."

"We . . . we got no choice, do we?"

"Not really."

"I got some twine," Allison said.

Gambrel scowled at him. "What the hell are you carrying twine for?"

"What the hell do you care?" Allison snapped back. He knelt beside his one of the packs that were thrown on the floor and quickly produced a ball of stout twine.

"That should do," Longarm said. "Now turn around an' give me your hands. I'll see if I can get you out o' here alive. Not that I really give a shit, but I'll see if I can do it."

The two very unhappily complied.

Chapter 39

As soon as the prisoners appeared at the doorway, the low rumble of the mob changed to a roar of fury.

"Baby killer" was perhaps the most common charge screamed at Gambrel and Allison. "Animal," "Piece of shit," and "Miserable cocksuckers" were also popular.

Gambrel and Allison cringed and shrank back when they heard the hate pouring from the throats of the townspeople. The good folk of Alvarez did not countenance child molesters. A dark stain appeared at Bobby Allison's crotch and spread down his right leg where he pissed himself. Longarm did not blame him. Hell, he might have pissed himself, too, had he been in Allison's place.

Longarm motioned for silence, a pistol in his hand. He had his own Colt in his holster and two revolvers he had taken from his prisoners, but if real trouble started, those would be of no more use than trying to empty the ocean with a teaspoon.

And he damned sure did not want to fire into the air to get people's attention. Any gunfire, no matter its purpose, was apt to set the mob off on an orgy of killing.

Quite apart from the fact that he had a moral obligation

to protect these bastards now that he had them, he did not want to be in the line of fire should violence erupt here.

"These men are my prisoners. They'll be tried for their crimes in a proper court of law an' then they'll prob'ly hang. But they'll hang legal, dammit. It won't be no lynching," he shouted. "Now where can I find your jail?"

Some of the men closest to him calmed down at least a little.

"You do have a jail, don't you?"

"Yeah. We got a jail," a barefoot man in a nightshirt and armed with a butcher knife admitted.

"That means you have a town marshal then?"

"Got a constable."

"Take me to him." Longarm prodded his prisoners forward. The mob reluctantly opened before them, flowing around them like water. Water that was still close to the boiling point, he thought. One careless spark could ignite them like a keg of powder. "Take me to your constable."

A man with a short-barreled shotgun in his hands stepped forward. "I'm Constable Jim Butler."

"Help me take these prisoners to your jail, Butler. We need t' get them off the street an' out of sight."

"All right, boys," Butler shouted to his neighbors. "Let us through there. Get back. Now dammit, Charlie, stand back there. Let us through. These men surrendered. Let us through."

The crowd—which no longer had the intensely ugly feel of a mob—split in two, leaving an alley walled off by men who were glaring but who at least were under control. Longarm and Jim Butler walked the prisoners through that gauntlet and back into the town.

The jail was little more than a shack itself. It had no bars, but it did have several U-bolts planted in stout posts

166

set deep in the ground. Chains ran through the bolts. Prisoners deemed a danger to run could be secured to the chain with leg irons.

"Just a minute here. I need to light a lamp and find my padlocks so I can put the irons on these jaspers," Butler said. "And by the way, who are you anyhow?"

Longarm introduced himself and said, "Thanks, Butler, but why didn't you step in earlier an' try to get that crowd under control?"

"Mister, I make thirty dollars a month in this job. For that amount, I'm not gonna offend all my friends and neighbors and risk dying, too. Especially not for a pair of pricks like these."

"Well, you're honest about it. Can I trust you t' watch over them while I get after the last o' the crowd? He has the little girl an' I wanta get her away from him quick as I can catch up with him."

"Like I said. I won't die for the bastards. But I will keep them here for you. Or you can take them along with you. Suit yourself."

The choices were piss-poor. If Longarm tried to find secure accommodation for his prisoners, he risked letting Roman Turner get away with Tina.

Not that there was anywhere—not in Wyoming or Utah or any other heavily Mormon area—where the laws of the United States could not be enforced. Turner was blowing smoke about that.

There were, however, some places in the mountains to the west where it would be hard to ferret Turner out. Places where neighbors did not talk about one another. Places where the sheer emptiness of the country made searching almost impossible.

Longarm did not want Roman Turner to reach the

mountains. He feared he might never find Tina if Turner had time enough to get that far.

Late as it was and tired as he was, Longarm wanted to get after Turner right damned *now*. And in order to do that, he pretty much had to trust Jim Butler to take care of Gambrel and Allison.

"All right. I'll leave 'em with you. I can't tell you when I'll be back for them, but the government will reimburse you for their keep while you have 'em. Is that all right?"

"Yeah, I suppose so."

"Jesus, Marshal, don't leave us here. Please, Marshal. Please don't be leaving us," Bobby Allison cried.

"I got no choice," he told the two. "But don't worry. You're in custody now. You'll be all right while I'm gone."

Longarm retrieved his horses, which were still fresh and ready to cover ground, and reined them west out of town.

He paused on a hill about three quarters of a mile beyond the jail. When he looked back, he felt a coldness in his belly and imagined he could hear the screams of two dying men.

The jail was aflame, the fire sending a column of smoke and sparks and ugliness high into the night sky.

Apparently Constable Butler had not done a whole hell of a lot to take care of those prisoners.

Not that Longarm had any warm feelings toward Bobby Allison and Nelson Gambrel. But the bastards had been his prisoners.

"Shit," he mumbled out loud.

Then he wheeled his horses back around to the west again.

Chapter 40

After he got beyond sight of the fire that was consuming Nelly Gambrel and Bobby Allison, Longarm pondered long and hard about his best hope of finding Roman Turner.

Tina being with him would complicate his plans. He would not want to be seen in towns, and he certainly could not take the girl on the railroad or a stagecoach. Turner would have to continue to travel cross-country, avoiding civilization as much as possible. And now he did not have his bloodthirsty companions to back him. Any dirt farmer with a shotgun and a strong sense of right and wrong could put an end to Roman Turner's plans for the future. One word from Tina and Roman could wind up a dead man.

He had to know that, and the knowledge had to effect his course.

Longarm thought the probable route Turner would take would be to hit the North Platte and follow it west. Almost to Fort Laramie perhaps. Even though he could not take Tina onto a railroad car, he would not want to stray far from the route of the Union Pacific. It was the only way to avoid the Big Horns.

Once he slipped through south of them, he would have a thousand choices about where he wanted to disappear.

Longarm needed to catch the bastard before he could get that far.

He thought about it. Then bumped the grulla into a little quicker pace.

Longarm came awake with a start. He jumped a little and had the sudden fear that he was falling out of the saddle. He grabbed hold of the pommel of his McClellan to steady himself, and shook his head to clear the cobwebs that infested it. He had been dozing off and on for the past two days, pushing the horses hard, stopping only when he absolutely had to.

He came awake now to find the red horse standing still. That was what must have wakened him.

The horse was stopped facing a tiny run of shallow water so narrow a man could jump across it without any trouble. The red horse, however, did not like to get its feet wet, and had to be spurred to get it into water. Once it was in water it was fine, but it hated having to step into moving water.

Longarm frowned and took a little tighter hold on his reins.

He heard someone laughing nearby. That would be the first human he encountered since daybreak.

He glanced toward the sun—his Ingersoll watch had long since run down—and judged it to be sometime in the late morning. Call it eleven or so.

Longarm had to look twice before he spotted a man squatting behind some willows. At first, he figured the man was in there taking a dump. Then he heard a calf bawl and smelled a wisp of smoke.

Interesting. There probably were a dozen good reasons

why a fellow would want to do his branding inside a tangle of willows when there was a hundred miles of open country in any direction around him.

A dozen maybe if he worked at it real hard, but the only one Longarm could think of offhand involved a running iron and somebody else's bovine. He reined the red around in that direction.

"Mornin'," he said.

The rustler stood, a sheepish look on his face. "Gave m'self away, didn't I?"

Longarm grinned. "Yeah. I guess you did at that."

"You gonna turn me in, mister?"

"No. Maybe I otherwise would, but I'm in something of a hurry an', hell, I don't know who that calf belongs to nor where to find him. You're getting away clean this time."

"I got to admit that that's a relief, mister. Say, you look pret' near wore out. I got a little coffee here if you'd like some."

"Friend, I would damn near kill for a cup o' coffee right now."

"I got some cold biscuits, too, and 'lasses to dip them in. They ain't much, but you're welcome to share."

"Thanks." Longarm stepped down off the red, took a moment to hobble both animals, and stripped his saddle and bridle off so the horses could graze and roll while he was eating.

He hunkered down beside the small, nearly smokeless fire. The rustler, a thin young man with blond hair and a scraggly mustache, had built it of dried cow dung. A cow chip fire will not have coals enough to burn a permanent brand, but it is enough to make a hair brand.

"If it's all the same to you, mister, I'll not give you my name. Reckon you can understand why."

Longarm laughed. "I don't mind giving mine." He stuck his hand out to shake. "Deputy U.S. Marshal Custis Long," he said. "But you can call me Longarm."

"Oh, Jesus! I'm fucked, aren't I?"

"No, I told you the truth. I have no intention to take you in. Hell, I wouldn't know where t' take you if I wanted to. Say, you make a damn fine cup of coffee. Better'n middlin' biscuit, too."

"I didn't bake the biscuits. My, uh, friend did that."

"Friend? Is that what they're called these days? My oh, my, I just can't hardly keep up with all this modern terminology."

"Truth is, we aren't married. Her folks didn't want her having nothing to do with me, so the two of us run off."

Longarm looked at the calf, lying hog-tied beside the fire, and he laughed again. "I can see why they might have reservations 'bout your character."

"Oh, that. You see we're trying to start us a homestead. We haven't had the time nor the money to get proper married. But we surely will. She's, uh, she's pregnant, so I don't think her old man will gainsay us much longer."

"Just as a wild guess," Longarm said with a grin. "Is that one of her father's calves layin' there?"

The boy only grinned back at him and shrugged. "Another biscuit and a little more coffee?" he asked.

Longarm felt almost rested by the time he stood, stretched, and picked up his saddle. "While I think about it," he said, "have you seen anything of a man and a young girl traveling west?"

"Funny you should ask about that," the young man said. "When I drug this here calf down into my favorite coulee thinking to have my branding party there, I found there was already somebody camped there. A big man with a bushy black beard and a young girl with hair like my wife's but chopped real short. So short she could pass for a boy, I think, except when I seen her"—he blushed—"she was washing herself. It was pretty clear then that she was a girl. Not real big, though. I, uh, didn't get all that good a look at her face."

Longarm could well imagine why the cowboy would not have been looking at her face. It almost had to be Tina, though. Roman must intend to pass her off as a boy. That would be why her hair was cut short.

Longarm's expression turned to stone. "Tell me where you saw them."

"Yes, sir."

Chapter 41

Longarm got down on hands and knees and crept up the hillside. When he neared the crest, he removed his Stetson and bellied up the rest of the way.

It was just like the young fellow said. There was a tiny seep of potable water, a stand of crack willow and bull-berry, and two people seated beside a small fire.

Roman Turner was a big sonuvabitch. He carried a Win-chester Yellow Boy and had a skinning knife on his belt.

The other person . . . Longarm had to look long and hard, and even then he was not entirely sure if the smaller person was a boy or a girl. Certainly, she, or he, was dressed like a boy.

If it indeed was Tina, then Roman had done a good job of disguising her. Apart from the short haircut, she had on jeans and a flannel shirt with the sleeves rolled up, shit-kicker boots, and a wide-brimmed hat.

If indeed it was Tina.

While Longarm watched, she took the coffeepot, emp-tied it, and then poured a little clean water in. She swirled that around and dumped it out, too. Getting rid of the cof-fee grounds, Longarm figured. Cleaning up.

Roman said something to her, and Tina nodded. She shook the last drops out of the pot and put it into a pack that lay open on the ground. Turner kicked dirt over what was left of their fire.

He said something more, and this time Tina shook her head. She cringed away from the big man, but he grabbed her wrist and yanked, pulling her onto his lap.

Longarm had no desire to watch any more of this shit. He picked up his hat, stood, and walked down the sharply slanting slope into the bottom of the coulee.

Turner did not see him coming, but when Longarm was twenty feet or so from them, Tina did.

There was no longer any doubt that these two people were Roman Turner and Tina Washburn.

The girl jumped to her feet and screamed, "Uncle Custis!"

Turner leaped up, too. He took hold of Tina and dragged her to him, using her as a shield.

Billy Vail would have been proud of Longarm. For once, he remembered to do things by the book. "Roman Turner, I'm placin' you under arrest," he shouted.

The dumb son of a bitch who wrote that book obviously knew nothing about the real world. Turner responded by pulling his knife and laying the cutting edge against Tina's throat.

"Back off or I'll kill the kid," he warned.

This was the same man who slit Teddy-something's belly open and left him to die slowly. Longarm had no doubt that he would cut Tina's throat, too.

"Lay that pistol down," Turner said. "Slow. Ease it out of the leather and put it down easy, Uncle Custis." He laughed. "It's funny, ain't it. All this time this fucking kid's been saying that her Uncle Custis was gonna get us. Said we should've let her loose. I thought she was telling fairy tales to scare us into letting her go. Now here you be. Did I mention that you'd better lay that gun down or else?"

Longarm thought about it. If the cocksucker did use his knife, Longarm would kill him as sure as the sun rises.

That would do nothing to help Tina, though.

If he did as Turner said and dropped his Colt, Tina might have a chance to get out of this alive.

As far as Longarm could see, the only firearm Roman Turner had was his Winchester, and that was lying on the ground a good ten feet away from where Turner had Tina now.

Roman had the skinning knife, of course, and that was as deadly as any firearm could be.

Still and all . . .

"All right. I'm laying it down now."

"Slow. Use your left hand. No, not the pistol. The belt. Unbuckle that belt and drop it. Slow and easy-like."

Longarm carefully unbuckled his gunbelt. He had a moment's impulse to palm the Colt and put a .44 slug through Roman Turner's forehead. There was no question that he could do it. He could have a bullet smashing through Turner's brain in a split second.

But how quick was Turner? Could he in that same amount of time pull the blade of his knife across Tina's vulnerable neck?

From where Longarm stood, he could see the pulse fluttering in the little girl's throat. Her skin looked as thin as parchment. It would take so very little to cut through that big artery that ran along the side of the neck.

It was not a risk Longarm was willing to take.

He let the gunbelt fall to the ground.

Chapter 42

"Now, you pissant piece of shit," Turner roared, "now let's see who puts who under fucking arrest." He let go of Tina and gave her a shove, sending her sprawling.

Longarm ducked down, but Turner was already on him, bowling him over, driving him to the ground, driving the breath out of him.

Turner was on top of him, one knee in Longarm's belly so that he could not breathe. The knife swept down to deliver a death blow.

Longarm grabbed Turner's wrist. Stopped the descent of that wicked blade.

It took every ounce of strength he possessed to keep that knife from finishing what Roman Turner intended.

Longarm strained against the big man's force and while he did so, he tried to suck in some breath.

He could feel the lack of air begin to overwhelm him. His vision blurred and turned gray.

Just inches above him, Longarm could dimly see Roman Turner's gloating expression as he anticipated the sight of Uncle Custis's blood spurting high in the air like a bright red fountain.

Longarm gathered what strength he could for one last attempt to shove Turner off him. If that failed, however—

A long, black spot like a rod or a poker came into view above Longarm's face. Pushed past the hand that held the knife to rest against the front of Turner's shirt.

Longarm could not see well enough to recognize what it might be. The world swam in shades of red and he was close to passing out from lack of air. The knife blade—

He heard a muffled bang, and the front of Turner's shirt burst into smoldering flame.

The big man grunted and fell backward, rolling off Longarm and falling onto what remained of the coals from his lunchtime fire.

Blood gushed out of Roman Turner's open mouth and his eyes glazed over. His mouth worked as if he was trying to speak, to say or to ask something. Whatever it might have been never got spoken.

Longarm sucked in one long breath after another. When he felt up to it, he sat up and turned his head to see.

Tina was there. She was sitting cross-legged on the ground in her boy's clothing and boy's haircut. She was crying. Roman Turner's Winchester lay across her lap.

"I didn't . . . I didn't . . ."

"It's all right, baby," Longarm said. "You did good. You're safe now."

"But I . . . I . . ."

"You did the right thing, sweetheart. You lived through it. It's behind you. It was just a bad dream. You hear me? It was a bad dream. All of it."

Longarm stood. He picked up his gunbelt and buckled it around his waist where it belonged, then reached down to Tina.

The child took hold of Longarm's hand and he helped her to her feet. "They . . . those men . . ."

Longarm shook his head. "Hush now. Those men, all of them, they're dead. They can't hurt you no more, and no human person on the face of this earth needs t' know what-all you had t' do in order t' survive. I won't be asking you an' nobody else needs to either."

He smiled. "It isn't too far down to the railroad, y'know. How's about you and me catch us a train. We'll take the easy way home. There's already been enough that was hard."

Tina wrapped her thin arms tight around Longarm and sobbed into his chest.

He let her have her time to cry. They were in no hurry now. None at all.

Watch for

HELL UP NORTH

the 365th novel in the exciting LONGARM
series from Jove

Coming in April!

GIANT-SIZED ADVENTURE FROM AVENGING ANGEL LONGARM.

BY TABOR EVANS

2006 Giant Edition:

LONGARM AND THE
OUTLAW EMPRESS

2007 Giant Edition:

LONGARM AND THE
GOLDEN EAGLE SHOOT-OUT

2008 Giant Edition:

LONGARM AND THE
VALLEY OF SKULLS

penguin.com/actionwesterns

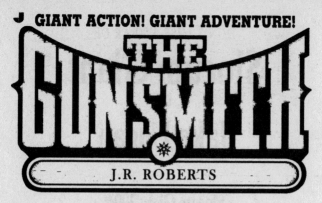

GIANT ACTION! GIANT ADVENTURE!

THE GUNSMITH

J.R. ROBERTS

penguin.com/actionwesterns

M228AS0808

DON'T MISS A YEAR OF

Slocum Giant
by
Jake Logan

penguin.com/actionwesterns

M230AS0808